IDEAS
of
HEAVEN

IDEAS
of
HEAVEN

A Ring of Stories

Joan Silber

W. W. Norton & Company New York London

Excerpts from *Gaspara Stampa, Selected Poems*. Edited and translated by Laura
Anna Stortoni and Mary Prentice Lillie. New York: Italica Press, 1994. Copyright
1994 by Laura Anna Stortoni. Used by permission of Italica Press. Excerpts from
Petrarch's Canzoniere or Rerum Bulgarium Fragmenta by Francesco Petrarch,
translated with notes and commentary by Mark Musa. Used by permission of
Indiana University Press. Excerpts from *The Selected Poetry of Rainer Maria Rilke*
by Rainer Maria Rilke, translated by Stephen Mitchell, copyright © 1982 by
Stephen Mitchell. Used by permission of Random House, Inc.

Manufacturing by Quebecor Fairfield
Book design by Chris Welch
Production manager: Julia Druskin

Library of Congress Cataloging-in-Publication Data
Silber, Joan.
Ideas of heaven : a ring of stories / by Joan Silber.— 1st ed.
p. cm.
ISBN 0-393-05908-1 (hardcover)
I. Title.
PS3569.I414 I33 2004
813'.54—dc22
2003024324

W. W. Norton & Company, Inc., 500 Fifth Avenue, New York, N.Y. 10110
www.wwnorton.com

W. W. Norton & Company Ltd., Castle House, 75/76 Wells Street, London W1T 3QT

1 2 3 4 5 6 7 8 9 0

For Myra

CONTENTS

ACKNOWLEDGMENTS

I want to thank Myra Goldberg, who read this manuscript more times than anyone should ever have to and always gave peerless advice. Andrea Barrett, Charles Baxter, Kathleen Hill, Margot Livesey, and Noelle Oxenhandler were also generous readers who gave crucial suggestions and support. I have been extraordinarily lucky in having Carol Houck Smith as my editor and Geri Thoma as my agent. Special thanks again to Sharon Captan for her friendship. I am grateful to the MacDowell Colony for a residency during the writing of this book.

"The High Road" appeared previously in *Ploughshares,* and won the 2003 Cohen Award from *Ploughshares.* It is included in *The O. Henry Prize Stories 2003* and *The Pushcart Prize, XXVIII: Best of the Small Presses.* "My Shape" appeared previously in *The Story Behind the Story: 26 Writers and How They Work,* ed. Peter Turchi and Andrea Barrett (New York: Norton, 2004).

IDEAS
of
HEAVEN

MY SHAPE

I had my own ideas about a higher purpose, but not enough ideas. I could have used more. When I was in my early teens, I used to go to the bus station in my city and think about panhandling money to get a ticket to Las Vegas. A wide sky of nightclubs glittering in the middle of the desert sounded beautiful to me. I wanted beauty. I'd sit on a bench and do my homework in the bus station, and then I'd go home.

What did I want before this? I took ballet lessons twice a week in the gym of my grammar school and liked the arabesques and the leaping and even the strictness of Miss Allaben drilling us in the six positions. I worked hard at ballet until I began to grow a figure in my leotard. My other hobby was attending services in churches and synagogues all around Cincinnati, where we lived. My parents were a mixed marriage (Jewish and Catholic, a big

13

deal then) and had solved the alleged difficulty of this by not following any religion.

So I was a fascinated tourist in any house of worship, and
would go anywhere I could get taken. The whole notion of
worship knocked me out. I saw Jews kissing their fingers and
touching them to the velvet cover of the Torah, I saw Catholics
kneeling with their mouths open in practiced readiness for the
Host, I saw Greek Orthodox placing their lips on icons as if
they could not bear to pass them without this seal of adoration.
I would emerge blinking into the daylight, shocked at my
friends' laughter over what had gone on in there—the choir-
master's bad haircut, the tedium of the sermon, the utter
ridiculousness of somebody's mother's hat. I listened, harder
than anyone else, to words never said in daily conversation—
beseech, transfigure, abounding, mercy. The rapped chest, the
bowed head, the murmured Dear Lord. I could not get over
people doing this together, the gestures of submission that went
on within these walls. Then the congregation got up and
walked outside.

Since no one—not my friends or family or even the clergy
themselves—seemed to take this to heart the way I did, I had to
keep quiet, like a spy with encoded notes or a tippler sipping a
flask in the ladies' room. I made up perky reasons for wanting to
go each week, "just to see how people are really all alike." After a
while, I heard myself making fun of it with the others, and I
stopped going. All at once, suddenly, cold turkey. I turned my
back on the whole thing.

So. Then I grew the mounded body that was to be my adult shape. I came from a family of women with large breasts, and by fourteen I had my own set, which I sheathed in satin brassieres that made them point forward in military cones. Torpedo tits they were called (by us girls too). Everyone knew that grown men became entirely helpless at the sight of cleavage, the compressed hills rising gloriously above a strapless gown. This fashion in bodies has faded, but I was glad of it then. It is true that in junior high the boys yelled dirty comments (they mooed like cows, they made milking gestures with their hands), but I believed that these immature oafs, as we called them, liked me.

By the time I was out of school, everyone seemed to be telling me that I might enjoy certain privileges if I played my cards right. Once that idea got unpacked, it was more complicated than I guessed—what these privileges were and where contempt hid in the granting of them and what had to be paid for them anyway. People think they know all about this now, but they don't, not exactly.

I wanted to be an actress. I was too silly and shallow to be any good at acting, but I could keep my composure onstage, which is something. I was given small parts in summer stock, the hooker or the stenographer or the cigarette girl in the nightclub scene. The summer after my first year of college, I worked in the Twin Pines Theatre. I slept with the bullying director, a fierce-browed man in his forties who had sex with a lot of us and didn't give anybody a bigger part for it. Sleeping your way to the top is a bit of a myth, in my experience.

I liked acting, at that age. You got to dwell on feelings, which were all I dwelt on then anyway, and turn them over, play them out. We had long discussions: would a child afraid of her father show the fear in public? would a man who was in love with a woman talk more loudly when she entered the room? Those who'd had real training (I was not one of them) spoke with scorn about actors who "indicated," who tried to display a response without actually feeling it. An audience could always tell. What was new to me here was the idea that insincerity was visible. I understood from this that in real life I was not getting away with as much as I thought.

But otherwise I was a little jerk. I was so hungry for glamour that I put a white streak in my brown hair, I wore short-shorts and wedge heels, I drank banana daiquiris until I threw up. I thought the director was going to find himself attracted to me again and we might have a legendary romance, although I could hardly talk to him. I didn't know anything.

One of the other women told me about a job on a cruise liner. If I could dance a little, which I was always saying I could, I might be one of the girls strutting around in sequins in the musical revues they put on to keep the passengers from jumping overboard in boredom. I could get to Europe, to the Caribbean. They didn't pay you much but you ate well.

The woman who told me this was the director's new cookie, and I was not sure what she was really saying to me and in what spirit. We're artists, you're the showgirl, etc. But perhaps she did want to give me something.

And I worked on cruise ships for years. I went to Nassau and Jamaica and Venezuela and through the Greek islands. I worked in clubs in Miami too, walking around with a big feathered head-dress on and the edges of my buns hanging out the back of my satin outfit. I lived with a bartender who was irresistible when he wasn't a repetitious, unintelligent drunk, and with an older man I never liked. I was twenty-seven—getting old for this stuff—when I got work on a ship going through the Mediterranean, along the French Riviera and Monaco and Liguria.

It was a French ship and that was how I met my husband, who was the ship's purser. He was a soft-eyed man with a whimsical blond mustache, who looked wonderful in the white uniform of the cruise line; everyone on the ship had a crush on Jean-Pierre. He was really just a boy. He was older than I was by a year, and he had poise and good sense, but he was not very worldly. I seemed to dazzle him, which was certainly nice. And I fell for him, his genial flirting and his down-and-dirty ardor in bed.

There is an hour on any ship when twilight turns everything a bright and glowing blue and the horizon disappears, the sea and the sky are the same. The line between air and water is so apparently incidental that a largeness of vision comes over everyone; the ship floats on the sky, until night falls and everything is swallowed in the dark. I have memories of being very happy with Jean-Pierre while standing out on the lower deck in that blueness, before the ship's lights came on. He asked if I looked like my mother or my father, and if I was close to them (I certainly was not). He wanted to know if I could ever live away from my family and my country for good, if I had ever thought of such a thing, and I saw myself moving toward a destiny as interesting as any I could have wished.

I had very little to leave behind, when I went with him to live in St-Malo, the ancient walled city in Brittany where he had grown up. Jean-Pierre acted utterly proud to have nabbed me. When he introduced me to people, he always repeated my name, *Ah-lice,* with a certain delighted pause before it, and his translations to me included goofy compliments no one had really said ("my cousin says you are the flower of America"). We were staying in an apartment that belonged to his uncle, two doors from a fish market whose scent I did not even mind. We married a month after he brought me there. It was a pretty town, high on a bluff, but it had been bombed badly in the war and not all of it had been built back. The rainy beaches were filled in summer with dogs and children running around on the sand. Signs insisted it was *strictement défendu* to bring unleashed dogs anywhere on the premises, and I was amused to see that none of its citizens paid attention.

His family was not unkind to me either, despite the fact that I tried their patience with my meager French and seemed dopey to them in general. Their friendliness was to ask me about Mickey Mouse and Elvis Presley, and in the childishness of these questions my language skills got better. At the endlessly long family dinners on Sundays, I could yammer my answers.

I had a running joke with Jean-Pierre about all the idioms English speakers have for anything sexy or duplicitous—French kisses, French leave, Frenching the bed, French ticklers. We were pretty jolly, the two of us. When we went back on the ship together, I was full of rich confidence. I beamed at the corny banter of old men and their wives, I danced like a proverbial house on fire. I wrote letters to my family from our ports of call, Corsica, Sardinia, Malta. *Allo, chère maman*, I said, I'm having more fun than I can tell you. *Je t'embrasse*, from Alice the blushing bride.

After Easter, when we went back to St-Malo, the town was full of tourists from other parts of France, and I would chat with them across the tables in cafés. People there didn't do that, but I thought they should, and I got them going. In the winter, when Jean-Pierre was hired for another tour of duty, there was no job for me on his ship, and he said maybe I could just stay home without him this once. I had worked since I was nineteen, and this offer of leisure seemed wonderful to me.

But I went a little crazy, by myself like that. I was no longer a novelty to his family and they had conversations I could not follow. In the dank and icy months, I walked around in a heavy, dressy cape and told the children I had a gun underneath it; I told Jean-Pierre's mother she was so cheap that she fed us horsemeat; I tried to hitchhike to Rennes but I came back after fifty creepy kilometers on the road with a dead-silent truck driver. Once I got drunk and stood on a table in a café, singing "Blue Monday" and looking down at the patrons. By the time Jean-Pierre got back, I was mopey and fat; I had gained twenty pounds. I had become a thing the French really hate, a blowsy woman.

What could we do then? We fought, quite nastily. He seemed

stuffy and spiteful, not like someone I knew at all. He said everyone had told him I was a selfish baby but he had said, oh, no, I
was devoted to him. We made up and spent two days straight in
bed (our desire never cut so deep as then). We went on excur-
sions to Caen and to Mont St-Michel, which even I knew was a
famous abbey, although I had stopped caring about churches. We
walked across the causeway to get there, and that was the part I
liked, walking into the sea. We gave parties for his friends and I
made American foods—fried chicken, coleslaw, macaroni salad.
The wives began to think I was a big, loose, amiable fool. Jean-
Pierre got work in a shipping firm in St-Malo.

For my thirtieth birthday we went to Paris. I had never been
there before, and much of it thrilled me—the cake-like elegance
of the buildings, the determined verve of people in the streets—
and me, Alice, walking through it with my handsome French
husband. But I felt too, in the thick of those groomed and confident crowds, the discomfort outsiders often know in Paris, the
dawning sense that this is not, really, for us at all—we will never
be this stylish or this knowing.

I came back to St-Malo in an agony of thwarted hopes. I
thought that all my prettiness, all the gifts I'd been so pleased to
have, had gotten me nothing at all. What did I want so desper-
ately? What in the world is *glamour,* what did I mean by that? A
heightening of the ordinary, an entry into the club of splendor, a
feast of endorsed sensations? Whatever it was, my anguish in
wanting it was almost more than I could stand. I suffered blindly.
Dolly of silly notions that I was, I wept real tears.

I knew I couldn't stay there weeping. I wasn't bound or indentured, it was the twentieth century. But I wept like that for another year—a shrew to Jean-Pierre and a puzzle to the town. I had one affair, with a humorless older cousin of his, and Jean-Pierre had lovers. In the end, I took the train to Paris and got a cheap ticket on a charter flight, and I left—after weeks of ugliness with Jean-Pierre's family (I might have handled that part better). I went to New York to dance and sing in Broadway shows.

What was I thinking? That it was my last chance. I had never been to New York, and I didn't know how to go about any of it. I showed up for one audition and waited in an outer room crowded with women much younger than I was. In the studio, I could keep in step, when they had us copy a sequence of dance moves, but I was not really dancing. I could sing on key, but in a watery, underpowered warble. I sang "Je Ne Regrette Rien," which made the casting people smile wryly.

This did not make me want any of this less. I thought I had never worked hard enough for anything before (this part was right). *Being in a show* seemed like the exalted professional use of the body, the gold spun from sweat. In *Variety* I saw an ad run by a man who coached performers for musical auditions—twenty years' experience, proven methods. I was so happy after I called him—I was taking charge of my life, as I meant to do. I walked back to the Y where I was staying and I celebrated by eating a steak at the coffee shop next door. I can remember chewing it happily, sitting alone at a table in private joy, putting little charred pink-brown bits of it on my fork with the baked potato, reading a *Vogue* magazine as I ate. I liked food in America.

I was late getting to the coach's the next day. The studio was on Tenth Avenue, farther west than I'd been before, and I had not realized how far this was from the subway.

"Should I bother with you?" he said when he opened the door. "What do you think?"

"Oh, yes," I said, tittering and dimpling. "Please."

He was a tall man who had probably once been handsome; he was stark and sinewy now. His dance studio was on the sixth floor of an office building, and the room smelled of old wood and mildewed drapes. I had to display myself for him. That is, I had to strip down to a leotard (I did this in a corner, awkwardly sliding out of my skirt) and follow him in a few dance steps, then perform them again while he looked glumly at me. Next he sat down at the piano and asked me to sing "Three Blind Mice."

"You remember that one, right?"

I tried to carry it off as jauntily as I could. Then he had me sing "Frère Jacques," which I at least did with a decent accent.

"Not much of a singer, are you?" he said.

I shrugged cutely, but I was very miserable. "I can be a dancer," I said. "Don't you think?"

"Maybe. How much do you want it?" He glowered at me from over the piano, a scratched black upright with a hoarse tone.

I answered that question with so much fervor that he smiled, a thing he rarely did, as it turned out.

His name was Duncan Fischbach and I was to spend many

hours in his studio. At first it was like any dance class—he demonstrated some steps, and we did them together, and then we linked a few of these sequences, which I was supposed to remember. "Listen to me, are you listening?" he said. "The word *oops* does not get you anywhere in this world, no matter how big a rack you've got on you."

I laughed a little. Women did not take umbrage in any club I'd worked in.

"I hate a giggler," he said. "Do it again till you get it right."

I did the steps again. He circled around me, checking. "Your balance is bad," he said. "Stand on your right foot and don't move until I tell you."

I stood for as long as I could, swerving and dipping and regaining my center. "You have to do better than that," he said.

I had to jump in place for fifteen minutes without losing the beat. I had to run around the room and change direction on a dime. I had to hold a number of positions for long spells of time—a split, a high kick, a stretch to my toes with my butt in the air. All of them were exposing, implicitly sexual positions, and I felt like a crude cartoon, twisting and straining, muscles trembling. Nonetheless I was proud of my discipline in the regimen this strange *maître* was drilling me in. And I did get more limber.

At my age I had no chance of getting anywhere, Fischbach said, unless I practiced at least seven hours a day. Minimum. I could not do much in my closet of a room at the Y, so I paid to use Fischbach's studio in the evening hours. I was given a key, and I went into that room, with its old-gym smells, always afraid

that he was going to appear, but he did not. My body grew
lighter and trimmer. I was skipping meals to save money, as the
savings I had brought with me ran lower. I had taken a vow to
myself not to look for other work. I was so lonely my voice
cracked from disuse when I spoke, but I was elated too in a
starved and ghostly way.

Sometimes I went to shows (or halves of shows—I walked in at
intermission, the one way to go for free). Things had been changing in the theatre; the hit shows of the decade were *Hair* and *Jesus
Christ Superstar*. They were okay, but I liked the older ones better—*Gypsy, Guys and Dolls, Oklahoma*—an earlier style of full-
throated, tip-tappy entertainment. Most musicals gave me
pleasure, but it was not a fan's love for them that made me knock
myself out. I saw them as a way to be in a parade of dazzling
motion, to be a lovely dancing version of myself, without the raw-
ness of the clubs. The best of me (I believed) was in that lineup,
slim-legged and tight-waisted, too delightful to keep under wraps.
That parade, which is always passing through this world, was
what I was made for, I thought. I could not bear to have it go by
without me. It hurt me to think it might have slipped by already,
that I might be too old. I probably was too old.

Fischbach had other students. A few times I met women going
in or out, girls with pearly lipstick and pixie bangs. Never any
men. I couldn't tell what his own desires were, which gender he
liked, or whether he couldn't stand the thought of doing anything with anybody. There was no gallantry in him—the tools of
his trade were mockery and command—and he was uncharmed

by femaleness in general. He was a strong dancer himself, not miraculously light on his feet but muscular and sure; his lines were always clear. He called me an oaf, a potato, a slob, a blight, a hippopotamus.

He believed in tests for me, rehearsals of my resolve, as if the strongest desire had to win, simple as that, in any instance. "Pop quiz," he would say. "If a director asked you to stand on your head with a dead fish in your mouth, what would you do? If someone stepped on your hand in the middle of a number, how would you act? If you were in California and had to get to a performance in New York and no planes were flying, what would you do? If your grandmother wanted you to stay at her bedside in California, what would you tell her?" There were no trick answers, but the recitation of responses was my practice in "mental clarity."

Sometimes I called France collect and talked to Jean-Pierre on the phone. The life I'd had there seemed cushioned and soft, a child's tented garden. When Jean-Pierre was friendly (sometimes he was not), I would get off the phone and shed tears. I would sit in my room at the Y and have to talk myself back into doing my exercises. How had I, who had once been loved and had a home, thrown myself into this pit?

This could not go on forever. Fischbach had forbidden me to go near any audition until he said I was ready, but I had had thirty-six sessions with him. Week after week. On Labor Day weekend he was going away (did he have friends? it was hard to imagine) and he would do a special extra-long class with me before he left on Friday afternoon.

I was a little late, and he said, "I might have known. Do you have any idea at all what traffic is going to be like this afternoon? Any clue at all?"

"I'll dance fast," I murmured brightly.

This was the wrong joke to make, because it gave him the idea to have me do routines in double time. He hammered at the piano with his fingers angled like claws. I was beet-red and sweating heavily when we stopped.

"Now that you're warmed up," he said.

He took up a wooden yardstick from the corner. For a second I believed that he was going to hit me with it. "You know the limbo?" he said. "Did the frogs limbo in your part of La Belle Frogland?"

He held the stick out stiffly, like a traffic gate. "Under," he said. "Lean back. Go with your pelvis first."

I had done this before, as a teenager in Cincinnati. "Oops," I said now, as I bent my knees and cakewalked under the ruler, my shoulders and head going last. It had been much jollier with a line of guffawing kids and calypso music on the hi-fi.

"Again," Fischbach said.

He lowered the stick. I wriggled under. The silence was not pleasant.

"Again," he said. The move meant thrusting my private parts at him—that was the whole comedy of this game—and for once I was not happy to be doing that. Fischbach kept his face impassive; he looked stony and perhaps a little bored.

"Again," he said.

I had to spread my knees wider to keep my footing.

"Again," he said.

I tried to angle one hip lower and twist my torso under the stick, which made me lose my balance. I righted myself by holding on to Fischbach's arm. "No," he said, and shook me away. I skidded and landed hard on my tailbone.

"You didn't last very long," he said.

"Yes, I did."

"Stay, don't move. I have floor work for you."

He walked to the far wall. "Okay," he said. "Come to me. On your hands and knees."

"What?"

"Just a little crawling. Fast as you can. It's a good workout. Don't argue."

I was going to argue, but then he told me not to. I thought I would just get it over quickly—I put my palms flat on the floor and I lunged and scuttled forward, like a swimmer in a race. My bare knees scraped the floor, but I kept thinking I was almost there. Soon, soon. This was a nightmare, but if I did what I had to properly, it would be finished.

"Very good," Fischbach said, when I had reached him. "Very nice. Don't get up, sweetheart."

I sat on the floor, cross-legged, waiting. *Sweetheart,* he said that?

"One last thing," he said. "Then you're ready." I actually nodded.

"Lick my shoe."

"What?"

"You need to do this. You pick. The right or the left."

He was wearing white canvas tennis shoes. I looked at his feet and I looked up at him. His face had almost no expression, but his eyes, in their hooded sockets, were fixed on me, to let me know that I had to do this. I respected (that is almost the right word) the clarity of his will. You might have thought we were both in the service of a great idea. For a moment I did think that. I lowered my head and I touched my tongue to the tip of his shoe, just once. The roughness left a dry spot on my tongue.

I was crying, of course, when I looked up at him. Not a mild flow of tears, but helpless, snotty sobs. Fischbach stayed poker-faced. He really did believe in some theory of severity and triumph, some grand dedication, but there was nothing at its center. He did not care whether I danced or not, or whether anyone did. There was no divine substance he was burning me down to.

While I was crying, I understood clearly that I was never going to be a dancer in any Broadway show. Not now, not later. I saw too that I didn't want it so much really. It was as if I suddenly remembered a thing that had been blocked by distraction and interruption. I sat on the floor in my soaked leotard and I was sick with disappointment to be someone who didn't want this.

My crying naturally disgusted Fischbach, although it could not have been a surprise to him, I could not have been the first to break down in his studio. (Unless I was the first he was able to push that far, a truly painful thought.) "Okay, okay. We're done," he said.

He went over and rolled the casing down on the piano keys. I could see that he was trying to carry out these last moments with what he thought of as style. "Get your stuff together," he said. "I'm in a hurry. Don't dawdle like you do."

He got his dungaree jacket off the chair and put it on, tugging at the bottom of it and turning up the collar. "Are you listening?" he said. "Move it. Chop-chop. It's time." He seemed pathetic to me, bossing around a woman who was stretched out on the floor in a fit of weeping. Where could that ever get him? I didn't move—that was my one tiny piece of resistance—and he said, "I'm waiting." He stood over me for some minutes. At last he said, "Never mind. You can lock up when you leave." I left the door open, in fact, and I never mailed him the keys either.

AND SO I went back to Jean-Pierre. He met my plane in Paris, and he looked wonderful to me, with his soft eyes and his cropped sandy hair, his topcoat flapping in the wind. He seemed very happy to see me, and he didn't rebuke me or ask me terrible questions. Later he was less kind. His family never treated me with any warmth after I came back.

Everyone did notice how slender and strong I was. I could not explain to them how I had stretched and kicked and *plié*'d and tied myself in knots in that stuffy studio, tearing and rebuilding the muscle fibers, pushing myself past the threshold of strain. Once I was back in Brittany, those hours in the studio seemed heroic—*I* seemed heroic, in my submission to the regimen, my single-pointed efforts. And for what? For a vision that was laughable even to me and had made me come back ashamed.

But I did come back a less silly woman. I did not plague Jean-Pierre about things he could do nothing about. And I tried to keep up my training. I would put on a record of *Wonderful Town!* and strut across the kitchen floor to Rosalind Russell. My niece and her friends, who saw me through the window, wanted me to teach them. I began to give lessons to little girls in "jazz dancing" and also tap, which they requested. I liked children and might have had them with Jean-Pierre if we had gotten along better. I could get my class looking like a line of Shirley Temples, all shuffling-off-to-Buffalo in their patent leather shoes, merry and mostly in step, and afterwards I helped them on with their little coats.

When the class got too big for any room in our house, I rented a room in the *mairie,* where the town's municipal offices were. It was quite a grand room, with molded plaster garlands along the ceiling and a nice parquet floor. It tickled me to have "The Pajama Game" pouring through its august spaces. Adults wanted to come too to the class, so I had an evening group of solid housewives and lithe young office workers and even a few men. I was a fad, perhaps, but people had fun.

I could not have lived on what I made from my dance classes, but they kept me afloat. Some girls came year after year, and their sisters too. Every fall I worried I wouldn't have students, but I always did. And I was allied with what Americans used to call physical culture. I went hiking in the valley of the Rance, I went to Paris for yoga weekends. Jean-Pierre laughed the first time he saw me in hiking boots; he said I looked like a Valkyrie in shorts. I liked my muscles more than he did, and they weren't ungainly either. The littlest girls used to beg me to show them a *grande jetée*—and I could jump and land without much thud or bobble even in the later years. The classes were the best part of my week. When Jean-Pierre fell in love with someone else and we split up at last, I was not altogether at a loss. I had something I could do, an occupation. I could not, however, stay in the town.

I went to Paris, to brood and idle for a few weeks before going home to the States. It was not a happy time. I was appalled to think my marriage really was broken forever and I was sorry for the messes we had made. I walked through the whole city of Paris, from Sacré-Coeur to Montparnasse, from the Chaillot Palace to the Jardin des Plantes, trying as hard as I might (not hard enough) to keep from stuffing myself with food and drinking a whole bottle of wine every night. I chatted too much with waiters and ticket-takers and all the people in my yoga class.

We were doing the shoulder stand in yoga when I kicked someone behind me by mistake. He was a very polite Parisian in his late forties, who told me not to worry for a single second, it was good for his health to get clipped in the jaw now and then. I was not usually that clumsy. We whispered back and forth about how this was a more dangerous sport than soccer, but at least (he said) you didn't have violent yoga fans. After class he took me out for a very good lunch.

I liked him right away, most people did. He was a history teacher in a *lycée*, a widower with a grown son, with an interest in Zen Buddhism and Duke Ellington. I stayed in Paris because of him—Giles was his name—one week longer and then another week. People say Paris is expensive but you can get by if you know how. After it was plain that I was not going to leave the city anytime soon, I began to teach beginners' classes in the yoga studio. I was living with Giles by then in the 7th *arrondissement,* in an old apartment with a rocky sofa and an armoire as big as a stable.

We had a simple, almost rustic life. In the evenings we stayed in, without TV or too much outside company; we read and we listened to music. On weekends we had *pique-niques* in the park when the weather was good, or we played long, companionable rounds of honeymoon bridge. You might have thought we were old people, except that the sex was frank and lively. Quite lively.

Sometimes in the early days I went with him to talks by one of his Buddhist teachers, although they never really seized my imagination. I did learn to meditate, and the followers were certainly a smart group. Giles never pressed any of his enthusiasms on me, except for a habit of buying me cheap Japanese sandals, which he insisted on liking. How could a person scold him? He was always able to consider the most outlandish idea without arguing and was unshocked by anything I told him.

Ten years after we first started living together, I went home to the States to visit. My family made a fuss and then ignored me. I had become one of those ex-pats who didn't know who David Letterman was and who held her knife and fork like a European.

When I flew back to Paris a week early, I told everyone I was never leaving France again. Giles's son called me *la convertie*.

At the yoga school we always got a number of Americans in the classes, and I could see they envied my unfazed command of this city and its folkways. It amused me that I of all people had become some worldly personage with good bearing and a forthright gaze, like a type out of Henry James.

I might have turned out a lot worse. I tried not to be vain around the students, not to be some fluttery old bird in drawstring pants. I worried about Giles's health, which was not as strong as it might have been. Otherwise my complaints were truly minor. When Giles had a heart attack last summer, I came to know clearly what minor was.

I was not always good during his illness. In the hospital, I cried out when I saw the tubes clamped over his nostrils. On my visits, I held his hand and gazed at him, while everyone else chattered to him in their usual voluble way. In our apartment I didn't want to answer the door or the phone. I wouldn't go outside at all, except to visit Giles. People came to check on me—Liane, the head of the yoga studio, and Giles's son and his wife. "Get up now," Liane said. "Get yourself dressed." What a nuisance I was to everyone, what trouble.

When Giles came home again I was better. I cleaned myself up, I cleaned the house. I nestled on the couch with him, I brought him cups of *tisane,* I went out to shop. And I went back to teaching yoga, which helped me greatly. The difficulty of certain poses was especially useful. I had to concentrate and I had to be exact. Giles himself got lively again within a few weeks and claimed he felt the same as before. Better even.

In the months right after he was ill, when I'd begun working again, I began practicing a kind of Tibetan meditation called *tonglen*. In its later levels, you send relief and spaciousness, on your outtake of breath, to someone who has done you an injury. Naturally I picked Duncan Fischbach. I have never had another enemy. I'm sure no thought of me has crossed his mind for decades; I was one clumsy student among many for him. How our limits vexed him. He couldn't bear how little we could do. Broken athlete, he must be now, empty shell—who would need relief sent more than he would? I sit with my famous bust rising and falling as I breathe; he would laugh if he saw me. But I do think of him, in short spells and sometimes longer.

THE HIGH ROAD

My whole life, it always made me crazy when people weren't sensible. Dancers, for instance, have the worst eating habits. I can't begin to say how many anorexic little girls I used to have to hold up onstage, afraid they were going to faint on me any minute.

I myself was lean and tight and healthy in those days. I went out with different women, and I married one of them. I don't know why she married me, I was never kind to her, but women did not expect much then. She was probably a better dancer than I was too. I left her, after a lot of nasty fights and spite on both sides, and I went and had my life with men. It was a dirty, furtive, sexy life then—this was before Stonewall—but it had its elations. Infatuation, when it happened, could be visionary, a lust from another zone. From the true zone, the molten center of the earth. I was in my twenties, listening to a lot of jazz, and I thought in phrases like that.

Andre, my lover, was in fact a musician, a trumpeter with a tender, earnest sound, sweet like Chet Baker, although he would have liked to be as intense as Miles. Well, who wouldn't? I had been with men before him, but only one-night pickups, those flickering hallucinations that were anything but personal. When I met Andre, we were not in a bar but at a mixed party, and we had to signal each other cautiously and make a lot of conversation first. Andre was no cinch to talk to either. Other white people thought he was gruff or scornful but actually he was really quite shy.

When we went home together, after the party, we got along fine. For a shy person, he was confident and happy in bed (I was the rough and bumbling one). I could still recount, if I had to, the sequence of things we did that night. I have done them many times since—there isn't that much variety in the world—but the drama was particular and stunning just then. In the morning I made him a very nice breakfast (my wife had been a terrible cook) and he ate two helpings of my spinach omelet as if he could not believe his good luck. He had a dry sense of humor and he was quite witty about my makeshift housekeeping and my attempts at décor, the white fake-fur rug and the one wall painted black. We put on music and we hung around, smoking cigarettes and reading the paper all afternoon. Just passing the time.

I was working in a show on Broadway, skip-skipping across the stage in cowboy chaps and swinging my silver lariat, and he came to see me perform. I suppose the other dancers knew who he was to me. Backstage everybody shook his hand and asked him if it wasn't the dumbest musical he'd ever seen. The girls told me later how nice he was. And sometimes I was in his world, when we went to hear music in the Village or once up to a club in Harlem. Anyone who saw us probably thought I was just some white theatre guy wanting to be hip. Had we been a man and a woman, we would have had a much harder time walking together on the street.

Andre stayed with me more nights than not, even if he didn't live with me. But he had to go home to practice. A trumpet is not an instrument that can be played casually in someone's apartment. His own place, up in Morningside Heights, was in the basement (a great cheap find), and he had rigged up a booth lined with acoustic ceiling tile and squares of carpeting for his hours of practice. His chicken coop, I called it, his burrow. I never stayed over with him and I only visited him there once, but I liked to imagine him hunched over his horn, blowing his heart out in that jerry-built closet.

He wasn't getting gigs yet, but sometimes he sat in with musicians he'd met. To this day, I couldn't say whether he was a great player or not. When he was playing with anyone, I worried like a parent—I looked around to see what people thought. He was okay, I think, but so modest and unflashy that he could be taken for a competent dullard. But he had a rare kind of attention, and sometimes, the way he worked his way in and the way he twisted around what they'd been playing made the other players smile. He was just learning.

In the daytime, he worked as a salesman in a men's clothing store in midtown. Once I walked in the door and pretended to be a grouchy rich man who needed an ugly suit to wear to divorce court. Something hideous, please, something you wouldn't wear to a dogfight. This cracked Andre up. He laughed through his teeth, hissing softly. That's how bored he was there. He introduced me to the manager as his crazy friend Duncan, this lunatic he knew.

He was quite a careful dresser, from working in that place. A little too careful, I thought, with his richly simple tie and his little handkerchief folded in his pocket. I used to tell people he ironed his underwear, which he stoutly denied. For Christmas he bought me a silk shirt that probably looked silly on me but felt great. We had dinner that day with two of Andre's friends, Reg and Maxmilian. I made a goose, a bird none of us had ever had before. We kept goosing each other all night, a joke that wouldn't die. Reg got particularly carried away, I thought. Andre teased me about the ornateness of my meal—the glazed parsnips, the broccoli *polonaise*—wasn't there a hog jowl in anything? He wanted the others to be impressed with me, and they sort of were. Andre asked me to put on the record of *Aida* he liked, the one with Roberta Tebaldi.

"Renata Tebaldi," I said.

"Rigatoni Manicotti," he said. "What do I care what her name is?"

But I took to calling him Roberta after that. Just now and then, to needle him. Pass the peas, Roberta. Like that.

We were at the Village Vanguard with a couple he knew when

I said, "Roberta, you want another drink?" He turned his beautiful, soft eyes on me in a long stare and said, "Cool it."

I did cool it then, but not for long. He was sleepy in the club, since he had been working at the store all day, and at one point he slumped back in his chair and dozed. Anyone who noticed probably thought he was on drugs. I sang into his ear in a loud, breathy falsetto, "Wake up, Roberta."

The week after this, he refused to take me with him when he went out with his friends. He announced it at breakfast on Saturday. "You don't know respect," he said. "Stay home and study your manners."

He wouldn't say any more. He never got loudly upset as my wife had. I couldn't even get a good fight going.

"Go," I said. "Get away from me then."

But that night, when the show let out, I took off my satin chaps and rubbed away the greasepaint, and I went walking up and down Bleecker Street, checking out all the clubs that Andre might be in. I just wanted him to be sweet to me again. I wanted to make up. I walked through dark crowded cellars, peering at tables of strangers who were trying to listen to some moody trio. I must have looked like a stalking animal.

What if he never came back to me? He wasn't in four places I tried, and at the fifth, I sat at the bar and drank a scotch, but I couldn't stay still. I walked all the way to the river, close to tears. I had never seen myself like this, wretched and pathetic. I could hardly breathe, from misery. I just wanted Andre to be sweet to me again. I couldn't stand it this way.

On the pier I picked up a guy, an acne-scarred blond in a baseball jacket. I didn't have to say more than hi, and I brought him home in a cab to my place in the West Forties. He was just a teenager—the luxury of a cab ride impressed him. I could see he was less excited when we got to my neighborhood with its hulking tenements. My block looked gloomy and unsafe, which it was.

And there on my stoop was Andre, waiting. I was still in the cab paying the driver when I saw him. The boy had already gotten out.

Andre's face was worn and tired—perhaps he had been sitting there a long time—and the sight of us seemed to make him wearier still. He sighed and he shook his head. I put my arm around the boy and I walked him past Andre to my front door, where I fished for my key without turning around.

I could hear Andre's footsteps as he walked away—east down the street, toward the subway. I did not turn my head at all. What control I had, all of a sudden. I who had been at the mercy of such desperate longing, such raging torment.

When I got the boy inside, I made him some pancakes—he looked hungry—and then we fooled around a little, but I wasn't good for much. He fell asleep, and I got him up at dawn and gave him some money. He didn't argue about the amount and he understood that he had to leave.

And what did I do as soon as he was gone? I called Andre on the phone. How sleepy and startled his voice sounded. I loved his voice. When I said hello, he hung up.

And then I really was in hell, in the weeks after that. I woke up every morning freshly astonished that Andre was still gone and that my suffering was still there, the deadweight in my chest. When I phoned Andre again, I got him to talk, and he was rational enough, but he wasn't, he said, "very interested anymore." His language was tepid and somewhat formal. "Not about to embark on another disaster," was a phrase he used in a later conversation. That time I told him he sounded like a foreign exchange student.

So we stopped talking. Even I could see it was no use. But he was never out of my thoughts, he was always with me. I would be on the subway and realize I had shut my eyes in dreamy remembrance of a particular scene of us together, Andre on his knees to me in the shower. How languorous and smug my expression must have looked to riders on the A train. How disappointed I felt when I saw where I was.

I might have gone to find him at work, but I knew how he would be with me. If he was frosty over the phone, he would be a parody of polite disgust in the store. I hated the thought of actually seeing him like that, and I didn't want to hear what I might say back.

I didn't really have many friends to talk to. I was late getting to the show a few times, from not really caring and from sleeping too much, and I was fined and given a warning. I was very angry at Andre when this happened. He didn't care what he had done to me. I went down to City Hall, to the Buildings Department, and I looked up the deed to Andre's building to see who the owner was. I phoned the realty company to complain that someone was playing a trumpet very loudly at all hours of day and night. I phoned again and gave them another name, as a different angry neighbor. I phoned again.

On the last of these phone calls a secretary told me that the tenant had been advised he could remain in the apartment only if he ceased to be a noise nuisance, and he had chosen to leave, without paying his last month's rent. I was quite satisfied when I heard this—how often does anything we do in this life attain its goal? And then I remembered that I didn't know now where to find Andre. I didn't have his home phone number anymore.

I wanted to howl at the irony of this, like an anguished avenger in an opera. How had I not known better? Well, I hadn't. There was no new listing for him in any of the boroughs. And he was not at his job either. Another salesman in the store thought maybe Andre had gone back to Chicago, where his family was. I didn't see him anymore, not on the street, not in clubs, not in bars. Not then, not later. Perhaps he became famous under another name. Who knows how his playing got to sound? Not me.

All these years later, I don't know if he is still alive. A lot of people aren't, as it has happened. But it may well be that he settled down—he was like that—and a long and sedate monogamy would have kept him safe, if he found someone early, and he probably did. I wasn't with any one person, after him. I didn't even look for such a thing. I went to bars and took home the occasional hot stranger, and I kept to myself a good part of the time.

For a decade or so I got work pretty steadily on Broadway. Those weren't bad years for musicals, but there was a lot of junk too. I was hired to slink around as a thirties gangster, to be jaunty with a rake in my hand as a country yokel, and to do a leaping waltz as a Russian general, clicking the heels of my gleaming boots. Only a few male dancers got to be real stars, like Geoffrey Holder or Tommy Tune, and I suppose for a while I thought I could be one of them. I had a strong, clean style and I was a great leaper. Nothing else anywhere did for me what that sensation of flying did. But my career never made its crucial turn, and then I got older than anyone wanted for the chorus line.

Which was not even that old. I was surrounded, however, by lithe and perfect young boys. Quite vapid, most of them, but decently trained. I was not even attracted to these children, as a rule. Probably I looked like some evil old elf to them, a skinny, brooding character with upswept eyebrows.

For a while I tried teaching in a dance studio, but I didn't get along with the director. She gave me the beginners' classes, and the students really didn't want any grounding in technique, they only wanted someone assuring them they could be professionals overnight. "Ladies," I would say to them, "get those glutes tucked in before you practice your autographs."

I didn't last that long at the school, and so then I tried going on my own as a coach. I put an ad in a few papers bragging about my years of experience and my secrets for imparting the skills of theatrical success. I knew now what people wanted to hear. And I did get phone calls. My students were ninnies, the lamest of stagestruck clodhoppers, but they showed up for lessons with brimming eagerness, and I made what you could almost call a living.

There was one man I was very drawn to, during this time. He was a stockbroker I met in a coffee shop, a balding boy in a beautiful suit who asked what I was reading in my newspaper. I took him to the Jersey shore for Labor Day Weekend. He was too quiet in the rented car on the drive out, and I had to work to keep the conversation up. We walked the boardwalk, being dreary together, and on Sunday morning we had a short but insulting fight over something he didn't want me to do in bed. He didn't really like me, past a certain point.

And I paid for that weekend too, for the rental car and the hotel on the beach and the dinners of steak and lobster tails. He was younger than I was but he might have chipped in. I remembered those expenses with some bitterness, when my pool of students began to drop that year. I had to borrow from anyone I knew just to get by.

In the end I gave up the studio, gave up the whole idea of teaching. I got a job in an agency booking dancers for clubs. Go-go girls, in spangled underwear and little white boots. I was the man the girls talked to after they read the classified and came into the office, nervous and flushed or tough and scowling. I sent them to clubs in the outer boroughs, airless caves in the Bronx with speakers blaring disco and red lights on the catwalk. My temper was so bad that people did what I told them, which was the agency's idea of sterling job performance. I was a snarling jerk in these years. Contempt filled my every cell; I was fat as a tick on contempt.

These were not good years, and my drinking got out of hand.

One night in a bar, a man threw a chair at me and split open my head. When I missed two weeks' work, the agency hired someone else while I was gone, and there wasn't much I could do about it. It was not a clean or soft business. With my head still shaved and bandaged, I went back to the bar, itching for more trouble, but instead I ran into a dancer I used to know in my Broadway days. We were too old to want to pick each other up, but when I complained of being broke, he told me about a job at the union, answering phones and filing, if I didn't think that was beneath me.

I did, but I took the job anyway. I used to say the work was bearable because of all those pert young boys who came into the building, but in fact I was in the back offices, hovering over ledgers, and, in later years, facing a computer screen. It was a painless job, a reasonable thing to do until I found something else, and then it became what I did.

I didn't go to bars after a while. We knew at the union how many people were dying, even before the epidemic unfurled its worst. Cruising had not been full of glory for me anyway, so I stayed home and counted myself one of the lucky ones. Staying home suited me. I read more books, and I had a few regular outings. I had brunch once a month with a few theatre people I still knew. Through the union I got tickets to plays and sometimes operas. And I helped out backstage at some of the AIDS benefits we sponsored.

In the early years a lot of big names pitched in at these benefits, but later too there were people who were impressive in rehearsals. I stayed extra hours one night to listen to a tenor with a clear, mellow voice—he was singing a cycle of songs written by a composer who had just died of AIDS. The accompanist was an idiot and they had to keep repeating the first song over and over. The singer was a puny, delicate boy, with pale eyebrows and colorless hair in a crewcut. He closed his eyes as he sang—not good form on stage, but affecting nonetheless.

During the break I told him to keep his eyes open, and he said, "Yes, yes. You're right."

"Your Italian sounds good though," I said.

"I lived in Rome for a year," he said. "It was my idea for Jonathan to set these poems."

The composer had been his lover—I knew this, someone had told me—and the tenor sang with a mournful longing that was quite beautiful. *Amor m'ha fatto tal ch'io vivo in foco*, he sang. Love has made me live in ceaseless fire. I myself had xeroxed the text for the programs.

His name was Carl and he was young, still in his twenties. Recent grief had crumpled his face and left a faint look of outrage around his eyes. I began to bring him glasses of water during his break and to keep advising him. *Look at the audience. Watch your diction.* He was quite professional about the whole thing, and he only nodded, even when I praised him.

He let me take him out for a drink after the next rehearsal. We were in an overpriced bar in the theatre district, full of tourists. He ordered a Campari and soda. "Isn't that a summer drink?" I said. It was the middle of February.

"It makes me happy to drink it," he said. "It makes me think of Italy." As I might have guessed, he had gone there to study voice and he had met his lover Jonathan there. "The light in Rome is quite amazing," he said. "Toasty and golden. Too bad it's so hard to describe light."

He was a boy romantic. Every day he and Jonathan had taken a walk through a park with a beautiful name, the Dora Pamphilj or the Villa Sciarra or the Borghese Gardens, and they had poked around in churches to gaze at Caravaggios or had sat eating gelato in front of some ravishing Bernini fountain. I knew only vaguely what all this was. He glistened and pulsed liked a glow-worm, remembering it. I did not think any place could be that perfect, and said so.

"It's not," Carl said. "It can be a nightmare city. Noisy, full of ridiculous rules and only one way of doing things, and those jolly natives can be quite heartless. But because Jonathan is dead, I get to keep it as my little paradise."

"*Il paradiso,*" I said, dumbly, in my opera Italian.

He asked me if I had ever toured when I was a dancer. "Only to Ohio and Kentucky," I said. "Nothing exotic. I just remember how tiring that road travel was."

"What keeps me going," he said, "is poetry. I make sure to have a book with me at all times."

I pictured him reading a beat-up paperback of Whitman while everyone else slept on the tour bus. But his favorite poet, he said, was Gaspara Stampa, the Italian whose sonnets I had heard him sing. "She's sort of a 1500s version of the blues," he said. "Love has done her wrong but she's hanging in there. She thinks all women should envy her because she loves so hard."

I was an undereducated slob, compared to him, but one thing about being a dancer is you know how to pick things up. "I like that line you sing," I said, "about how I'll only grieve if I should lose the burdens that I bear."

"Yes," he said. "Exactly."

I WENT TO more rehearsals. I didn't scold or correct and I said "bravo" or "*stupendo*" when he was done. I patted him on the arm and once I hugged him. We talked about Verdi, which I at least did not sound like a fool about, and about the history of New York office buildings, and about what he had to do to keep his voice in health. I did not ask, really, about his health.

"I am all fire and you all ice," he sang. I told him they were torch songs. "Gender reversals of the traditional Petrarchan sonnet," Carl said. "A woman bragging about her unquenched longing. Very modern." What a swooner he was, how in love with pure feeling. And he was a huge hit at rehearsals. He had a theory about this too. "No good words are said anymore," he said, "on behalf of torturing yourself for love. Everybody's told to *get over it*. But a little bleeding is good."

I had noticed that hopeless passion was still in high style in certain corners of the gay world, but I kept this observation to myself. "The pianist needs to practice," I said. "You know that, right?"

I wanted to cook for him, this flimsy little Carl, and I got him to come for dinner on a Sunday night. "Whoa," he said, when he saw my tenement apartment, which had been carved out of the wilderness almost thirty years before. "You've got everything packed in, like a ship." For supper I fed him beautiful food that was good for his vocal cords, no dairy or meat, only bright and cooling flavors. Blue Point oysters, cold sorrel soup, prawns with pea shoots and fresh ginger, purslane and mint salad. Everything vibrant and clarifying. Golden raspberries and bittersweet chocolate for dessert. I had knocked myself out, as he could not fail to notice.

The food made him happy. He said that when he first came to New York, he had been so poor he had eaten nothing but tofu and Minute Rice. Even now I had to show him how to eat a raw oyster. I felt like his uncle. That was not who I wanted to be.

"This is as good as food in Italy," he said. "In my Surviving Partners Group there's a guy who's a chef. I'm sure his food isn't better than this."

"Surely not," I said.

His Surviving Partners Group met every week. It was a great group, he said. But for him personally what was most helpful was meditation.

"Eating is good too," I said.

"Yes," he said. "I forgot how good it was."

A beautiful suspense hovered around the table when he left for a minute to go off to the bathroom. When he came back into the room, I stood up and I put my arms around him. He was so wispy and slight, much shorter than I was. He ducked his head, like someone sneaking under a gate, and he slipped right out of my arms.

He did not mean to mock me, he had only been embarrassed. Neither of us moved. I felt old. A vain old queen, a self-deluded old fruit.

I asked if he wanted coffee and we sat down and drank it. He praised my espresso so lavishly that I couldn't tell if he only felt sorry for me or if he was trying to be friends nonetheless, if such a thing were possible with a grotesque old lech like myself.

AT THE NEXT REHEARSAL   Carl waved when he saw me. He came over and told me about how much better he sang ever since he'd eaten my dinner. "When I do my vocal exercises now," he said, "my voice is so good I move myself to tears." I thought he did like me. And perhaps I had not allowed him the time that someone like him needed. Perhaps the situation was not entirely hopeless.

When I went home after rehearsal, I lay in bed musing about what might happen between us after all. If I were patient. He had not been with anyone since his lover died and I had not been with anyone in years. I had underestimated the depth of the enterprise, the large and moving drama involved. He would probably have to make the first move. He would surprise me, and we would laugh at my surprise.

In the middle of the night I got up and looked at the condoms in my night table drawer to see if the dates printed on the packets showed they were past safe use. I threw out the one that was expired. I sat on the edge of the bed in my underwear, hunched over, with my head buried in my hands. I had never asked Carl what his HIV status was. I was ready to go to bed with him without any protection at all, if that was what he wanted. All those years of being so careful I wouldn't risk going out of my own living room, and now I would have bargained away anything to have Carl. I was beyond all reason.

AT WORK the next day the phone rang, and it was Carl inviting me over for brunch on Saturday. He was ashamed to cook for me, he said, but he could buy bagels as well as the next person.

He lived in a remote and dull section of Queens, on a street full of what had once been private houses. He had a nice little back apartment, with a view of the yard. "Welcome to my monkish cell," he said.

It was not cell-like—it was quite cozy and bright—but I was spooked by the shrines in it. On a small table, spread with a white linen cloth, was a collection of photos of his dead lover, who was a pleasant-looking young man, dark-haired and stocky. Jonathan waved from a deck chair on a beach, he stood in front of a Roman ruin and a bright blue sky, he laughed against Carl's shoulder at someone's birthday party. In another corner was an altar to the Buddha, with a stone statue of a thin, pigeon-chested Buddha facing into the room, and a fatter, calmer Buddha embroidered into a square of fringed brocade hanging on the wall. A single deep-blue iris, pure and wilting, stood in a vase. I did not like any of it.

But Carl had clearly wanted me to see it. He gave me a tour of all the photos, naming every guest at the birthday party. He gestured to the Buddhas and said, "Those are my buddies there." He told me that he did Vipassana meditation, adapted from what they did in Burma and Thailand, but that was a Tibetan *tanka* on the wall. "Very nice," I said. "It's the medicine Buddha," he said. "That's his healing unguent in the bowl in his hand." I chewed my bagel and nodded.

I gossiped about the rehearsals, just to get us somewhere else. "Did you see," I said, "how Brice is ogling that first violinist in the quartet? I expect him to drool all over the man's bow any minute. It's not subtle." Brice was the show's organizer.

"I missed it," he said. "I'm bad at noticing who's after who."

"Brice is so obvious."

"What can I tell you?" he said. "I'm away from all that. It's not in my world."

What world was he in?

"People don't think enough about celibacy," he said. "It hasn't been thought about very well in our era. It has a long history as a respected behavior. It has its beauty."

I knew then that he'd brought me here to say this, with the fittings of his cell as backdrop. "The Buddha never had sex?" I said. "I thought he had a family."

"That was before he was the Buddha."

"Don't get too carried away. You know you'll want someone sometime."

"I don't think so."

"It's *unnatural* at your age."

"I'm not unhappy."

Oh, honey, I thought, I didn't tempt you for a second, did I?

"A sexless life will ruin your voice," I said. "I'm not kidding. You'll sound like some wan little old lady. You already have to worry about that."

"Oh," he said. "We'll see."

"You already have some problems in the lower register."

"Oh," he said.

"You'll sound like a squawking hen in a few years."

"No more," he said. "That's enough."

I WAS DEPRESSED after this visit, but lack of hope didn't cure me either. I didn't stop wanting Carl, and what I wanted kept playing itself out in my mind over and over. At home I would sometimes be slumped in an armchair, reading a book or watching TV, and not even know that I was lost in reverie, until I heard myself say out loud, "Oh, honey." It was terrible to hear my own voice like that, whimpering with phantom love. I was afraid I was going to cry out like this at my desk at work, with other people in earshot, but I never did.

We were civil with each other at the last rehearsal. Actually, Carl was more than civil. He made a decent effort to converse, while the string quartet was busy going through its number. "I read," he said to me, "that Rome is all different now because they've banned cars from parts of it."

"You know what I read?" I said. "I read that there was a man who was very high up in a Buddhist organization who went around sleeping with people and giving them AIDS. Lots of young men. He knew he had it and he didn't tell anyone he slept with. He thought he could control his karma."

"Oh," Carl said. "That happened years ago. When did you read it?"

"A while ago."

"Why are you telling me now?"

"Those are the guys you want to emulate," I said. "Those are your shining models."

"No," he said. "That was one guy."

"Lust crops up," I said. "Can't keep it down."

"That's not what that story means," he said. "It's about arrogance and delusion, not lust. He could have used condoms."

"Right," I said. "Sure. You'll be like him. You'll see."

He reddened then. I'd forgotten that his HIV status might be positive, for all I knew, which did deepen the insult. He shook his head at me. "Oh, Duncan," he said, sourly.

ON THE NIGHT of the concert, I dressed very nicely. I wore a slate-blue shirt, a beautiful celadon tie that Andre had once given me, a stone-gray sports jacket. I hadn't looked that good in years. I sat with some other people from work in a chilly section of the orchestra seats. The string quartet was first, playing a stodgy piece badly. I really did not hear anything until Carl walked onstage to sing Jonathan's songs. He looked pale as marble, an angel with a shimmering crewcut.

He had a few intonation problems at first but sounded lovely and sure once he got going. Jonathan had written him easy music, except for a few jagged rhythm changes "*Viver ardendo e non sentire il male,*" he sang. "To live burning and not to feel the pain." Wasn't it enough that I suffered at home? Did I have to come here and hear my beloved wail about the trials of the rejected? I wanted to shout in protest. I should not have come, I saw. Who would have cared if I hadn't come?

Then my protest and exasperation fused with the plaint of the songs, with their familiar trouble, and I had a bluesy ache in my chest that was oddly close to solace. I felt the honor of my longing. This idea did quite a lot for me. My situation, ludicrous as it was, at least lost the taint of humiliation.

When the songs were over, I was surprised when the applause did not go on for hours, but people seemed to have liked the pieces well enough. I was still in a faint trance when the concert broke for intermission. I stayed alone in my seat while the others milled around. The second half was a woodwind quintet I had never liked, and they did three numbers. When they were finally done, I moved through the crowd and found Carl in the lobby, surrounded by people clasping him in congratulation. "*Bravissimo,*" I said to him. "Really." He gave me a sudden, broad

smile—praise from me probably did mean something to him—
but he was busy thanking people.

I stayed around long enough to get pulled along with a group
that went out for drinks afterward. I did not ask if I could come,
and perhaps I wasn't welcome, but no one said so. We sat at a big
round table in a bar with peach-tinted walls. The accompanist,
whose playing hadn't been as bad as I'd feared, kept leaning toward
Carl with an excited attention that looked like a crush to me.

Carl himself was busy introducing everyone to a young giant
of a man who turned out to be the chef from his Surviving
Partners Group. "My very good friend," Carl called him.
"Duncan, you should talk to Larry about his food. You're the one
who'll really appreciate what he does."

"Oh, I will?" I said.

"*I* like food," someone else at the table said. "I like it all the time."

I was about to say, "Cooks who are fans of themselves tend to
show it," but then I didn't. I decided to shut up, for a change.
There was no point to my baiting anyone at the table just for
fun, in front of Carl. No point at all now.

But it was hard for me. I stayed sullenly quiet for a while, sulk-
ing and leaning back in my chair. When Chef Larry told a funny
story about his poultry supplier, I didn't laugh. When Carl talked
about a production of *Wozzeck* that he was about to go on tour
with, all through Canada, from Quebec to Vancouver, I didn't
ask when he was leaving or when he was coming back. I didn't
say a word. And when the pianist said he had been practicing too
much in a cold room and he complained of stiffness in his elbow,

I gave him a very good exercise he could do at home. I explained it without sarcasm or snottiness or condescension. I was at my all-time nicest, for Carl's sake, for Carl's benefit. I don't know that he, or anyone, noticed.

CARL WENT ON tour for six months, as I discovered from his phone machine when I called him later. It didn't surprise me that he hadn't said goodbye—I was probably someone that he wanted out of his life. Still I dreamed of his return. How could I not? When he came back, I would tell him how I had begun to think of myself as a celibate too, that I had moved toward a different respect for that as a way to be, and perhaps we could be friends now on a new basis. It made me happy to think of our new comradeship, his easy and constant company, his profile next to me at operas and plays. But I knew, even as I imagined our lively and natural conversations on topics of real interest to both of us, that my reasoning was insincere, only a ruse to win Carl to me in whatever way I could.

But since I could not talk to Carl, who was off singing to the Canadians, I was left with my own recitation of why I treasured austerity running in a loop through my mind. I was the captive audience for what was meant to disarm Carl. This was not the worst speech to be trapped with. It made the tasks I did in solitude—my exercises, my errands—seem finer.

The exercises were a particular annoyance to me. I had done exercises all my life (except for some goofing off during the

booking-agency years) but now I had arthritis, plague of old ath-
letes and dancers, in my knees and just starting in my hips. All
that hopping and turning and high-kicking had been hard on the
cartilage. I had to go through a full range of motion every day to
keep the joints flexible, which they did not want to be anymore.
Some of this hurt and I hated being a sloppy mover. But now,
swinging my leg to the side, I felt less disgraced by it. My routine, performed alone in my bare bedroom, had its merit and
order. An hour in the morning and stretches at night. I had my
privacy and my discipline.

Every Tuesday evening I went to a guy named Fernando for
bodywork. I lay on my stomach while he bent my knees and
hooked his thumbs into my muscles. The word ouch did not
impress him. He had been a dancer once too. "Stay skinny, that's
important," he said. "Good for arthritis, good for your sex life."

"Good for what? I can't remember what that is."

"You can remember, Dunc. You're not that old." Free flirting
came with his massages.

"I don't know," I said. "I like my quiet. A life of abstaining isn't
as bad as people think."

"So they tell me," Fernando said. "I do hear that."

"See?" I said. "There's a lot of it going around. It's an idea
whose time has come."

"For some. Maybe."

"I think I'm happier. Do you believe that?"

"Yes," he said. "That I believe."

I HAD NEVER been able to throw away the program from Carl's concert, and it lay on a small table near the door, where I saw it whenever I came in or went out. I would read over his name with a ripple of intimate recognition. A ripple or a pang, depending on my mood. The very casualness of its placement on the table pleased me.

I knew from the message on Carl's phone machine that he was returning from Canada at the end of September. Once he was home, I would call him, and at the very least there would be friendliness between us. The wait seemed very long. Thirty days hath September, and in the last week I went to movies every night to keep busy. I saw too many bad, raucous comedies and bloody cop movies. The only thing I liked was a biopic about neurotic artists in the twenties.

When I came out of it into the lobby, there was a crush getting to the doors, and a man in front of me said, "No one pushes like this in Toronto." I took it as a good omen to hear some word in the air about Canada. The man who spoke was not bad-looking either, nicely muscled in his T-shirt, and he held another man by the elbow to keep from getting dragged away by the crowd. It took me a second before I saw that the other man was Carl. His neck was sunburned and he had let his hair grow longer.

And Carl saw me. "Hey! Hello!" he said.

He acted perfectly happy to see me. Once we were all out on the street, he introduced me to his companion. Josh, the man's name was, and they had met backstage in Windsor, Ontario.

"And then what could I do? I just packed up and went with him on the rest of the tour," Josh said. "I have heard *Wozzeck* performed more times than any other human being on the planet. Berg is not that easy on the ears either."

"I like him," I said.

"It was great to have company on the road," Carl said. "You know how the road gets. You and I talked about that."

"Yes," I said.

"I had fun hanging out with the tour," Josh said.

"Are you back here for good?" I said.

"We're looking for a bigger apartment," Josh said. "I like Queens though. It's not how I thought it would be."

"Some people like Queens," I said. "Certain timid types like Queens."

"Don't mind Duncan," Carl said.

"We'll invite you over when we get settled in," Josh said.

"Whenever that is," I said.

ON THE SUBWAY ride home I was too angry to sit still. All those sweet-faced declarations, and look how long Carl had lasted as a holy soldier of celibacy. I felt that he had tricked me and that he'd had the last laugh in a way that made me writhe. *A respected behavior,* my foot. And I had been ready to tread the same path. I who had never taken the high road in my life.

When I got back to my apartment, I went to the phone and dialed his number. I wanted to ask him: Don't you feel like a fucking hypocrite? Do you know what a pretentious little jerk you are? The two of them weren't back yet, of course. They were probably at the subway station still waiting for the N train to Queens. The phone machine said: Carl and Josh aren't home right now.

I breathed heavily on the message tape for a minute, just to leave something spooky for them to listen to. And what would Carl have said to me anyway if I had been able to hammer away at him with hostile questions? *I took my chance when it was offered. Anyone would do the same.* There was nothing else to say.

I had a shot of bourbon, which did not calm me down. It made me want to kick something, but I wasn't ready to throw out my knee from an action that stupid. I had more bourbon, but I might as well have been drinking water. I sat there with my hand pressed against my chest, the way a dog paws its snout if it has a toothache.

I understood, after a while, that there was nothing to do but go to bed. I got out of my clothes, and I went through the set of stretches I always did before sleeping. I felt confused, because for so many months these had been like a secret proof that I was worthy of Carl. I had been consoled and uplifted by the flavor of his ideas mixed in with them.

STRESS WAS BAD for my bones, and I woke up very stiff. My knee locked when I tried to get out of bed. *Look what love has done to me.* I felt like a ham actor playing an old man. I had a hangover too, and it was still very early in the morning. I wanted to phone Carl, but in disguise as something menacing, a growling wolf or a hissing reptile. I was good at making different sounds. Let him be terrified, just for a second. But then he would know who it was. He would say my name, and I would keep growling or hissing. Duncan, he would say, is that you? Stop, please. Ssssss, I would say. Ssssss.

I was too old to do that, too old for that shit. Instead I ate my simple breakfast and had my simple bath and went out to do my simple errands. A plain and forthright man. I was so calm at the supermarket (who ever heard of someone with a hangover being calm while waiting in line?) that I wondered if the attitude I had developed in Carl's absence was now going to stay with me and be my support.

Perhaps I was going to beat him at his own game (or what had been his game) and become so self-contained that I never spoke to anyone. I could work at my job without much more than nods and signals. I could move through the streets and be perfectly silent, quiet as any monk with a vow. Then Carl would know just who understood the beauty of a principled life.

Oh, in the Middle Ages someone like me might have been a monk, one of the harsh and wily ones, but dutiful. I could be a monk now, old as I was. (I had been raised a Catholic, although not raised well.) I could enter an order the way forsaken young women used to, when they were jilted by lying men and wanted only to take themselves out of the world.

I don't know why these thoughts were such a great comfort to me while I waited at the supermarket with my cart of bachelor supplies. But I got through the day, and the rest of the weekend, without doing anything rash. At work on Monday I went about my business in my usual curmudgeonly way. I was in pain but I wasn't a roiling cauldron. I thought that once the worst of getting over Carl was done, his influence would linger in this elevated feeling about aloneness, just as Andre had left me with a taste for certain music, for Bill Evans and early Coltrane. I was doing well at the moment, better than I would have thought.

A MONTH LATER I knew differently. I was tormented by longings for Carl night and day. I hardly saw anything around me—sunlight hitting the windows of a building, a man sitting on a park bench, a kid walking in time to his boom box—without superimposing on it the remembrance of Carl and things he had said to me, the most ordinary things. In Sunday school when I was a boy, one of the Sisters had told us that the Benedictine rule said to "pray always." I had a good understanding now of how such a thing was possible.

This can't go on, I would say to myself (how many billions of people have said that?), but it went on for a long time, for months and months. Sometimes I called Carl's apartment, to see if the machine still announced he was living with that twinkie from Canada, but it always did. Fernando the masseur told me that the only way to get over him was to find someone new. I picked up a man in a bar who was stupid and dull, and that made me feel much worse.

Since I had not really known Carl that well, after a year his face did begin to lose its vividness in my mind—I had only a few shreds of encounters to hold on to. But it would not be true to say I forgot him. He was like a hum that was always in my ears. He was something that was not going to go away.

I never thought I would end up the sort of person who hoarded some cruddy xeroxed program as if it were an artifact from Tut's tomb. As if it were my job to keep the faith. I had become a fool for love, after all. You could say this served me right, but it wasn't the worst thing that might have happened to me. Not by a long shot. No, I was better for it. I understood a number of things I hadn't had a clue about before. Why Madame Butterfly believed Pinkerton was coming back. Why Catherine's grave was dug up by Heathcliffe. The devotion of these years improved me, and it burnt off some of the dross. I was less quarrelsome with other people and clearer with myself. My longing stayed with me, no matter what. Who could have known I was going to be so constant? It wasn't at all what I expected, and I had some work getting used to it.

GASPARA STAMPA

(1523–54)

There had always been three of us—my brother Baldessare, my sister Cassandra, and I. When my brother died, I wanted to go into a convent. He was only nineteen, gentle and smart. I thought I had had enough of the misery of this world. My mother was against my leaving her, and my sister said I was unsuited. They were right, but in the years after, I was sorry more than once that I had this life instead of a nun's life.

We lived in Venice, in a small house in the parish of the Saints Gervasio and Protasio, and there was a tiny roof garden where I used to sit. My brother died in the summer, and the roof was cool. Downstairs various members of my mother's family were talking, and boys who had studied with my brother in Padua came to visit. I didn't play any music while I was in mourning, but I heard the patterns of melodies in my head. That was mostly what I did. I worked out fingerings for the lute I wasn't holding.

But I got lonely up there. I wasn't used to being so quiet, and after a while the voices below lured me down. I wanted to see what everyone was doing without me. I came down and sat with them and listened to a ridiculous and moderately funny story my uncle was telling. The room, with its dark green walls and its dull red drapes, seemed cozy in its heavy way, as always. I was ready to be reasonable.

After this nobody had to beg me to go out at night with the others. I would sit with my sister and my mother in the gondola, with the purpled water of the canal around us, and I was glad enough to be going where we were going. What I liked was the way we were flattered when we got there. Old men clasped our darling little white hands to their chests, young men said extravagant, flirtatious things to us. Oh, they had been waiting, nothing gave pleasure without us, etc. A whole evening at a salon without decently played music can be very, very long. Cassandra was a somewhat better lute player than I was, but I had a better voice.

I was twenty but I still thought I had a chance of marrying. When I sang the lines from Petrarch, "And blessed be the first sweet agony/ I felt when I found myself bound to Love," I was full of yearning for an unknown agony. The room was thronged with men. None of them was about to marry me; I was from a family at the edge of their world, untitled and unmoneyed yet beautifully educated. Maybe one of these men might set up a marriage for me or Cassandra with some poorer cousin of his—that was what my mother hoped—but until then they were our audience. It wasn't strange that I should quicken with feeling for one of these men, under the circumstances, and maybe no one was surprised.

It was a Gritti that I first liked, Cesare Gritti. He sat next to me at the table one night and he made a small joke about the quail we were eating, had they flown right into the pot, the kind of thing one of my uncles might have said. I liked him for it. He was older than I was by a good fifteen years. Someone read a lackluster sonnet after supper and we whispered mocking remarks to each other. And when Cassandra and I sat in the corner and sang, he made everyone keep quiet. So the next evening I looked for him at someone else's gathering, but he wasn't there, and then I knew, by the weight of disappointment, that I was gone over into a new craving. I looked for him all week, whenever we went out, and when he was there, I brightened, and the evening was full of promise.

This went on for months. One night, he offered to take Cassandra and me to a small musical procession the next day at Madonna dell'Orto. In the afternoon he called for us, and, after a little quiet talking with me (he did not really have to say much), we went in his gondola to his own house, where Cassandra waited in a room below us while he and I went up to bed. What did I think I was doing? I had by then come to understand that I was never going to have anything unless I took it in this way. I had very little thought of resisting him. I was innocent but also wildly delighted that what I wanted was really coming to pass. The shock of what our bodies were doing left me more at a loss than I had expected, I who was the donor of this favor. He was tender with me, he tried to help me. I had not known that I was going to be thrown into a river of pleasure in which I could not swim or keep on course. How confused I was, in all my new and specific excitement.

Even then I would not have said we were in love, but we liked each other well enough. We met like this only one more time. He was hearty and gallant, as before, and I felt a new embarrassment at doing something so naked and intense with him. He was never unkind, but when he left for Milan, I was not sorry to have it over between us.

After this, when I went out to salons at night, I was livelier. I had been lively before—quick in conversation, eager to talk and display myself—but now the rooms looked different to me, more full of hidden heat. My mother used to hold salons, before Baldessare went off to school, and there were never more than a few women in the room, then or now, and none of them were wives. And if I was never going to be a wife, what was I going to be? My sister was afraid I was going to slip into one romantic alliance after another, but what I now knew made me careful for myself. I talked to everyone with greater ease, but I really was very careful.

I kept my wits about me in this way until I was twenty-six. On Christmas Day of that year we went to Domenico Venier's palazzo for a holiday gathering. We came in from the wintry cold and were escorted up the marble stairway, and at the top a very handsome, tall blond man came over at once and spoke to me about the singing we'd all heard in San Marco the night before. Any musician is cranky about performances, and I had opinions about how one piece had been arranged. He shrugged—he had liked the singing—and said what an extraordinary ear I had. Everyone was always praising me in some way—it meant nothing—but here I beamed and gushed and would not stop talking to him. His name was Collaltino di Collalto, and although plenty of first sons were given this kind of repeating name, I had to tease him and ask whether his parents thought people had to be told twice who he was. "Only you," he said. "Only you have to be forced not to forget."

"Are we talking about force?" I said. "What sort of man has to resort to that?"

"By force," he said, "I mean the power of true feelings. I mean giving in to joy, which is only natural."

"Anything natural shouldn't be called force," I said.

It was the sort of lilting debate people liked to have at these gatherings. Can love exist without compulsion? Can a man fall in love by hearsay rather than sight? Is it only a defeated love that leads to higher faith? What did Petrarch's Laura really look like two centuries ago? But in this particular private conversation the mention of *force* and *giving in* set up a reckless train of thought. He was not stupid, he must have seen. "Does it matter what you call an act?" he said.

"Yes," I said. "The name is what we remember things by."

We were very pleased at this beginning. We felt quite sharp in each other's company. He was my own age, a count from the mainland, from Treviso, and he had already been in battle in France. He talked to me with great eagerness, but then he was repeatedly drawn away to talk to other people, and it made me miserable each time. Whenever he came back to me, I was delirious with triumph.

During the music, which was longer for the holiday, with more instruments and more kinds of songs, I tried to stand near him when someone else was playing. We signaled each other with eyes rolled in dismay or nods after some of the madrigals. The best part of the evening was sensing the form of his body without looking directly at him. He was most purely mine then.

When I was home and lying in my own bed, with the bedcurtains pulled around me to keep in the warmth, I saw that I was close to sick with attraction. I was not as young as I had been with Gritti, and I knew enough to worry for myself. But I could not have kept away from my thoughts of him, my detailed imaginings. I had no other thoughts. My mind had nothing in it but Collaltino, a person I hardly knew. Can love exist without compulsion?

I saw him a few nights later, at another gathering. He came over to me at once, and said something conventional and enormously gratifying about how exquisite my face had looked when I was singing on Christmas. My cousin who was an abbess in Milan once wrote to me that if I wasn't wary of flatterers I would lose my own shining honesty. But I didn't think I had become corrupt, or gullible either. Collaltino was truly taken with me, in his lumbering and coolheaded way, and he hovered around all evening. I could see that he wanted us to come to an understanding. I only wanted him to love me, which seemed like a clear enough idea, but what did I mean by that? There was no future in what he wanted, but I was not, at that moment, thinking very far into the future. Only of my own thirst and how it might be slaked. My sacred thirst.

My mother was somewhere in the room, and she came over at one point and met Collaltino. He described an ice storm over his family's groves of hazelnut trees in Treviso, and my mother later said she had never heard anyone talk so well about the weather. My mother was still a pretty woman, and we resembled each other—the straight noses, the high foreheads—and Collaltino might have imagined my face in later years, if he had wanted to reflect on that. But probably he was thinking chiefly about what my situation was. My father died when I was seven, and my mother had an easy and impractical temperament. She was not a plotter herself but she was not going to stand in our way.

I was not totally lacking in sense, but my longing for Collaltino was so strong that his interest was a reward beyond anything I could pray for. I did pray for it too. He sent me a note, which contained some pleading and humble entreaty along with a bullying suggestion that Love, the most vengeful of gods, would punish us if we didn't heed him. I wrote that although I had not wanted such a letter, his pleas had made me pity him. We were mannerly but really quite straightforward with each other.

Our first time alone together was in his family's palazzo, on a February afternoon. I was late arriving, and when he greeted me in the hallway of his house, he looked eager and a little worried from waiting. It moved me to think of him waiting. I'd had a very cold ride on the water, and my hands were icy when I touched him, which made him shudder. He held them over my head while we lay on a divan, kissing, and one of his own hands (perfectly warm and solid) moved over me. I could not do anything but be his feast, a state I was thoroughly happy in, until he released my wrists.

And by then I was in a kind of swoon. I would have done anything he wanted, but what he wanted was perfectly simple. His lovemaking lasted longer than Cesare's had—he was stronger and had a greater appetite—and the numbness in the tissues afterward was like a glowing trace. I felt broken and quiet. We fell asleep, and when we woke up, he fed me a pear—he cut it and held the pieces out to me, the sort of thing I would have expected him to do, and yet it seemed exquisitely generous. He had me drink brandy, to warm me before I went out, and he sent me home in his gondola. I knew even then that I was at his mercy, but I felt cosseted and wealthy in it. When I came home, full of sunny phrases for what had happened, my sister said, "Petrarch never slept with Laura."

"Everyone knows that," I said. She meant that I would be sorry, but I was very far from that.

And I really was not sorry. For most of the winter, I had Collaltino's company at night in the salons, where I blazed and shimmered around him (my excitement was not a secret), and we had our afternoons, with their own luxuries. His bedroom, carved and gilded and heavily patterned and smelling of him, was the stage where our scenes unfolded, so rich (I thought) in private invention. Tullia d'Aragona, a women poet I admired, wrote that physical union, because it can never permit the total penetration of the bodies, can never satisfy the craving for union. But I thought that desire was a pure gift and not a conundrum. Collaltino was attentive and fond, he cried out my name, he laughed in amazement after the moment of climax. I was dazzled by most of it, this was a golden time for me.

I do not envy you, O holy angels,
For your exalted glory and great blessing,
Nor the fulfillment of your ardent longings
Always to stand before the face of God,
For my delights are such and so abundant
They cannot be contained in human heart.

I had not expected to be so overtaken by what I felt. I did see that sometimes he was silent when I was very talkative, and once when I ran across a courtyard because I was glad to see him, he stepped back and called out, "Slow, slow, Gasparina." His nature was firmer, cooler, less fluid than mine was. I knew that.

After our first few months he had to go back to his family's estates in Treviso. I had not known how hard it would be to be separated from him. It was at this stage that I began writing poems. He didn't send word by writing and I suffered a great deal. I was not ashamed to suffer openly. The acuteness of my own pain astonished and humbled me. Burning, piercing, binding, pressing: all those phrases were exactly true, exactly apt.

They were not metaphors, they were precisely what the heart in my chest was subjected to. It was an education to know myself in this form.

When Collaltino came back, he was glad enough to have me jubilant at the sight of him, and not interested in reports of tears. How vivid he looked to me, so much more *present* than the figure I'd had in my mind. The particulars can never really be held and saved, even by a lover. When I went home from our reunion in bed, exhausted and victorious, I thought of Petrarch, how he suffered, and how for twenty years he longed for Laura without ever living out that love. He made his home in the perfection of that yearning. I would rather (I was thinking) have what I just had. I would rather live in the particulars.

But I had these thoughts when I was happy. Collaltino kept going back and forth to the mainland, and when he was in Venice, he could no longer be counted on to be eager to see me. Once he summoned me to his house and was not there when I came. He had gone out to play chess with a friend and forgotten that he'd asked for me. I stayed in his room for hours, waiting, and then I had to summon his gondolier to take me home. The note I left was full of outrage and complaint and piteous begging, but nothing made any difference. "You could have waited a little longer for me," he said. I saw then (although I did not believe it) that I was going to become one of those who loved at a severe disadvantage. I had not thought I would be one of those people.

We quarreled bitterly when Collaltino told me (and he must have known for some time) that he was leaving for France, to be

there with his captain if fighting broke out with the English.
France! He had to join his company—anyone, he said, could
understand that. He was ashamed of me for speaking against his
obligation and he scolded me for crying in the street. He wouldn't
tell me when he was leaving, and he was gone from the city before
I knew it.

If it should happen, one far day, that Love
Should give me back myself, setting me free,
From this harsh lord—I fear, rather than wish it,
Such joy, it seems, my heart takes from its pain—
You will in vain call on my unsurpassed
Fidelity and love, immense, unbounded,
Repenting of your cruelty and error
Too late, when you shall find no one to listen.

What the poems did was make my lot plain to me. I had the
sense (whether I wanted it or not) that whatever I was carrying
had by now become a great love. It was embedded in me. I was
past being horrified and was in a state of some awe.

I slept very poorly after Collaltino left. He wrote to me a few
times, but then I had no word from him, week after week, and I
could only think of him wounded in battle and dying in anguish,
or in bed with another woman. I did not discriminate in my ter-
rors—they ran from the frivolous to the very grave.

It was easy enough to set any sonnet to music, and at night

when we went out to people's houses, I began to sing my poems. What I sang was what any lover knows: you'll be sorry later, I hope you feel one thousandth of the pain I feel, why are you so cruel. The stubbornness of these feelings seemed suddenly remarkable to me—an entire species beset by the same torturing wishes. The Platonists said we had an instinct for what could not be acted out fully in this world. People liked best the most mournful and complaining of my songs.

In the daytime I used to go out to the roof terrace to write. My mother had set out pots of lilies in the warm weather, and I thought of my cousin the nun sitting in her convent garden. When we first came to Venice, after my father died, I could not believe the city had almost no trees or greenery. My cousin's abbey outside Milan was cool and mossy, and the garden, which I had once seen, was at the center of a cross of pathways. I was trying to pretend I was in such a place.

It was hard for me when the season turned again and I had to go indoors. Then a letter came from Collaltino to tell me he was coming home. I had stopped thinking he was mine in any way, and the letter was startling proof that I had not dreamt him. Gaspara, he wrote, it has been much too long since you were in my bed. He wrote that: to me.

Oh, but the next week my sister heard from one of the Doge's advisers that Collaltino had done something very brave in battle (we didn't know what) and that his ship was not going to come back so soon as he'd said. When was it coming? No one could say. I had been patient for so long, and my punishment was not over.

I didn't know that he was ever coming back. My sister and my mother kept telling me to be more sensible, but I thought they wanted me to be a lesser person.

The valor of my lord, who steals the honors
From every other gentleman of valor
Is conquered by the sorrow of my heart—
A sorrow that outlasts all other griefs.
As much as he excels all other knights
In handsome form, nobility, and courage,
He is surpassed by my undying faith—
A miracle unheard-of save in love,
A grief no one believes who has not felt it—
Thus, I alone defeat infinity!

The one merit of this kind of waiting is that it can make whatever follows a wilder and more unbelievable pleasure. On a bluff day in November a man came with a note to tell me that Collaltino had just docked from the mainland with his regiment. I was not to go down to meet him, but he would send for me tomorrow, after he had seen his family. He would send for me, he said, as soon as he could.

The note did come the next day, and when I rode in the gondola to his house I felt that I was crossing the waters at the bottom of the earth, instead of simply going over the Rio di San Trovaso and along the Grand Canal. His palazzo, with the tall pointed arches of its windows and the wooden balconies, looked more sharply outlined than it had in all the times I had passed it without him.

When I saw him on the stairway, I tried not to rush at him, which he never liked, but I put my face against his neck. He asked if I had missed him, a selfish question with an obvious answer. I had a bad opinion of the war, and I didn't want all the bloody stories, and I was impatient to be in bed with him. But I asked how everything had gone in France, and then he began to tell me at length, which was not what I wanted.

We were sitting together on a cushioned bench in the central hallway. He spoke without much expression, and he listed places where his troops had surged or been cut off, places that meant nothing to me. I wanted him to say he had been thinking of me when the horror was at its worst, as I would have thought of him in any moment of extremity, but this was not part of his account. It was unspeakably small of me to be jealous of a war, but I was.

I got him talking about other things—things he had looked forward to being home for. I imitated our least favorite host, I half-recited someone's new poem, I listed what someone had served for supper. He was cheerful then, as he must have wanted to be, and we did go off to bed.

And once we began, his hunger for me was really very strong. If he had been with other women at the French court, and he probably had been, they had not drawn his deepest attention. He reached for me now like a man in a purposeful trance, and he did not seem to need to rest very long before his desire rose again. I did what I had not done before, I stayed the night. Before either of us could think of getting up from the bed, it was too late for me to leave; blue darkness was showing at the windows, and we were far out on our own sea anyway. We were awake still when the tint of daylight was seeping into the room, and Collaltino was very loving and playful.

When I came home, my sister said I looked just like the painting of St. Ursula where she is pale and leached of color from dreaming of her own death. "Saint? I would say not," I said.

"Stop laughing," she said. "You used to be so much calmer."

"I hate the calm I knew," I said.

O night, more glorious and more blest to me. I sang the poem about our night without any worry at all over what anyone said. Collaltino liked his tributes, and this might have been our best season, except that I knew he might go back to the war at any time. To cannon and gunpowder and danger. Collaltino didn't like it when I bothered him about my fears. He thought that I was unreasonable and shrill and unpleasant. Once I was sulky with him during a gathering at someone's house, and he wouldn't see me for a week.

And in a few months he did go back to France. It would have been easy for him to send word to me, but he rarely did. I prayed a great deal. That was all I could think to do. My mother teased me about praying *to* Collaltino—she said I had him confused with at least the Holy Ghost—but that was not my error. My sister used to tell me there were saints who described God in terms of carnal joy, and I had heard both my lovers call out the names of Christ when they were beside themselves. But I didn't make those mistakes. I kept the two realms of supplication as separate as I could.

What I wanted from prayer was consolation. I wanted God to come into the gap left by Collaltino. I thought that was the one thing I could ask of Him. Pour balm on my wounds, give me a space where thoughts of *him* won't enter. I was not offering repentance. I didn't see why any battle had to be fought over the field of my self, although I expected God to edge back when Collaltino arrived again.

There were poets who believed that the love of Collaltino might lead me to God, and it was true that I had some practice now in dedication. I might have gone further out of myself. I might have been a fool for Christ the way I was a fool for this man, but I didn't do it. I never did.

I dreamed, more than once, that Collaltino was with another woman in France. In one dream I had to watch him undressing for her. In another I waded into a swamp to reach him on the other side, but the bottom of the swamp was too deep and soft and the waters closed over my head. I woke up wanting to die.

I went on as I had. A count whose sonnets I'd heard at the salons asked me to join a poets' group, an academy where we read each other. I was pleased to be asked. We all took pen names, and I took the name Anassilla, for the river that flowed through the Collalto estates. My sister said I had made a costume out of my heartbreak.

This time when he came back he didn't send word to me, and my mother heard the news before I did. He went home to Treviso, and I lived on in a state of inflamed absence. A few weeks passed before he wrote in the friendliest way for me to come to him. How could I be so pleased and humiliated at the same time? But I went to him, to the family's castle at San Salvatore. His carriage took me, and I was tired when I arrived, but excited to see the stone fortress of his home, rising out of the hills, the woods all around it thick with pines and beeches. I had not really thought of him in the country. His brother Vinciguerra, whom I knew from town, came out with the servant to greet me. He said Collaltino was out hunting, he had planned to be back before now, did I want to rest and wait for him in the room upstairs?

My waiting in that room was like all of my time with Collaltino, a terrible compounding of delectable hope and enraged despair. I had fallen asleep in my clothes by the time he arrived. "Drowsy girl," he said. "Wake up, I'm here." Part of me had already given up on seeing him ever, and so the phantasmal sight of him caught me off guard, and I didn't even scold him. It seemed like such a stroke of luck to have him appear.

He kissed me tenderly for a long time, but stopped before we went further, and took me downstairs to have a light supper with his brother. For a little while I felt that we were really friends. We sat at the table, eating hot, savory dishes, and talking about whether it was natural to live in a city like Venice and whether a person who had never been outside it could imagine the peace of heaven properly. Or was a full idea of peace given to us at baptism? Collaltino said he had told his brother what an artful arguer I was. I thought that perhaps he and I had come through all our strife to be veterans of each other, familiar and fond.

He got up very early the next day to hunt for boar, and he had me get up with him, to breakfast downstairs before it was fully light. Why a man would come home from war to chase a wild animal with a spear was not something I could understand, and I didn't want to understand it. He was gone until sunset and by the third day of this I asked why he had wanted me to come to him, and he asked what good my education had done me if I was so unfit to amuse myself in solitude, and I shouted in outrage, and he imitated me, and then I really did pack to leave, but later he called me back so sweetly ("Why are you always leaving me?" he said) that I stayed for another week, and we quarreled through all of it. What did he want of me?

"You spoil everything by being indignant," he said. "You're making a joke of yourself, Gasparina."

He no longer even liked me much of the time, and I didn't exactly like him. This did not lighten my anguish. Other men had praised me while he was away, but what I wanted was Collaltino, why was that? An arrow shot at random had pierced my heart: this seemed perfectly true to me. I knew what he was, but my opinion made no difference at all. I was still waiting (how could I not wait?) for him to become something I could have.

Large streams of liquid, scintillating sparks
Burning and drowning me in fire and water,
Till not one grain of me is left
That is not turned to oceans and to flames—

Make him at least feel one among the thousand
Of these sharp pains that drown me and inflame me,
At least one flake of all the fire that burns me,
Or one small drop of water from his eyes.

When I came back to Venice from San Salvatore, I was tired and feeling frail, and within a day I was in bed with a fever. I couldn't go out to sing at the house of a man who wanted to be our patron, and Cassandra had to go without me. At home they fed me a white diet of delicate foods, pale grains and milky soups, but I couldn't eat. Collaltino was heard to say that he knew how I liked to play the sufferer so he wasn't too worried about my health. I was really very ill and the report of this brought me low.

In the night I was sick enough so that my family was frightened, and my mother and my sister kept watch over my bed. Who else but them? Collaltino had never visited our house and was not likely to. I lay shivering in my bedclothes, while Cassandra rubbed my arms and my mother gave me sips of water. I felt so sorry then for my brother, who had died in Padua without us. How terrible for him to be alone when his body was starting not to be his. My own body shuddered and pitched, as if it wanted to shake me off. The kindness of everyone was very moving to me, and yet I was lonely the whole time for Collaltino. I was weak and sometimes tearful, and I didn't even know which trouble I was crying for when I cried.

Then the fever broke, and I came to myself again. I was so glad to be in my own room, with the light falling onto the colors of the carpet. To sit up and take a cup of broth put me in a kind of rapture. I saw that I couldn't go back to the way I had lived, always suffering for Collaltino. What was the use of that anymore?

Collaltino wrote me a little note, to congratulate me on my recovery, and then he was genuinely surprised when I was angry with him. "Why are you so hard on me?" he wrote back. "What is it that you want me to be?" I said that he had never been anything but a rock of oblivion. A stone, a cliff. And then we did break it off between us. We were tired of our struggle, both of us.

I wanted only to be quiet, in the weeks right after. I was trying to remember my old life, when I had been reasonable and had taken a passing interest in all sorts of things around me. After I was well enough to be outside, I walked along the Zattere in the wintry light and studied the glints in the canal, and I did feel freer and lighter. But at night when we went out, people talked about Collaltino to me, and there was a rumor for a while that he might be marrying a viscount's daughter, but this turned out to be untrue. I still had my anguish in thinking of him, and a longing that stayed with me, like a secret faith.

IN THE BLEAKEST weeks in January, my mother took me and Cassandra to a very large and lavish party. Someone was reciting when we got there, and the play of pattern in the room—the brocaded taffeta hangings and the carved marble fireplace and the gilded and coffered ceiling—distracted me with a lovely giddiness. I felt a little drunk, walking into that splendor.

We had our lutes with us, but we didn't have to play until later. "How much I envy those souls chosen now," the host read, "to have her sweet and holy company." It was one of the poems Petrarch wrote after Laura's death. Why do we like to hear this? I thought. A man envying the dead. But I too liked it; it was exactly what I wanted to hear.

We had just barely finished supper when people started playing the Game of the Blind Men, a good game, really, and popular with this group. Each of the players had to tell how he had lost his sight because of love. The idea was to make the story as tricky as possible, full of obstacles and unflinching sacrifice, a set of tests. Rescuing the beloved from a fire, climbing the spikes of a fortress, crossing the Alps through the glare of snow. Lover after lover was struck in the eyes. Oh, why do we like to hear this? I thought, as we applauded the Alpine saga. We were all smiling, as if love's wreckage were a shared joke, which I suppose it was.

I went to congratulate the player who'd used snow and frostbite for his lover's trials. He shook his head and said, "The others were better." I wasn't accustomed to modesty in men. He was Bartolomeo Zen, quite high in the patrician lineage to be this affable.

"I remember your poems," he said. "I used to like them."

"I still write, I don't stop," I said. Everyone knew everything about me. "I write for occasions," I said. I still rewrote my old love poems, but I didn't have to say that. "Love isn't the only subject."

"I know that. People have lives around other things." He was looking across at Domenico Venier, our host, who was paralyzed and moved in a chair mounted on wooden wheels. Next to him were my mother, who had not been with a man since my father died twenty-two years ago, and my sister, who was a virgin. The three of them were congregated under a dark, misty painting of Venus and Cupid. Weren't they tired of being surrounded by nothing but the drama of desire? I had never heard any of them complain, although I had complained myself.

"Only in a convent or a monastery," I said, "could you pass a whole evening without anyone talking on and on about earthly love."

"Not even there," he said. "Everyone knows there are bawdy monks. And even the most unstained monks have some human interest in the subject. They're not infants."

"So there's no escape?" I said. "I don't want to think that."

"I would be very interested to read the newer poems," he said.

I TALKED ABOUT him when we got home. I thought Cassandra might know more about him. When had we met him before? Was he about my age or older? Zen, everyone knew of the family, but what kind of a name was that? "Shortened from St. Zeno," Cassandra said. "Don't you think? Patron of newborn babies, watch out."

She didn't know any more about it than I did. I got into bed and drew the curtains and went over the few things he had said, as if they were a tune I was learning. It was very pleasant to invent delicious scenes with him. But to be aroused was to think of Collaltino, and so I had both of them in my mind at once.

My father used to say, one nail drives out another. I thought of my breast hollowed out by one wound and bared to another. I had enough sense to be horrified, but this fear was very close to excitement. And what had I suffered for, these past three years, if all of it might have been for someone else all along? Hadn't I just spent an evening hearing about lovers so resolute they never turned back even when their eyes were put out? It was true that Collaltino and I had broken our ties, clearly and finally. I had no obligation to him. But week after week and month after month, I'd risen to my sufferings and been altered by them, been grateful for the alteration. Where was that understanding going now? I was leaving my faith.

But I was elated, fixed on this Bartolomeo, recalling the sound of his voice. What is Love doing to me? I thought. That question itself comforted me. So I was ruled by Love, his follower. Chosen to serve. I was like a priest being sent to a different parish.

THE NEXT DAY a servant came with a note from Bartolomeo, expressing his admiration for my gifts, his gratitude at seeing me, his hope that I might agree soon to have dinner at his home. He wrote quite well, with less bombast than Collaltino. I was not too jaded to enjoy reading the note over.

When I went to him the next night, my mother was upstairs in the back of our house, nowhere near the landing for the gondola. That was what she always did, kept away so that she could know without knowing. I had a sudden wish at that moment to be more like her, to be in my life and apart from it.

But I might not have been so afraid. Bartolomeo was really very easy to be with. He had a supper set out for us in a small, jewel-like room, and he led me into conversation with questions, the way a woman would. What time of day did I like to write? Did the time of day someone was born affect how long he lived? Did I look forward to the prospect of living to be very old? Were the Doges elected too old? He had more humor to him than Collaltino had. A small dog begged from the table, and he sent her away with what seemed to be a private joke between them about a morsel hidden under his shoe.

"I didn't mind her begging," I said.

"You'll meet her again," he said. "She'll know you when you come."

I THOUGHT ABOUT him so much after that visit that I wrote an acrostic for his name—no puzzle could have entertained me more—and he was pleased when I gave it to him. "It makes me love my own name," he said. He gave me a copy of Marcus Aurelius, in a very pretty dark red leather binding, as reading for the old age I'd said I was expecting. After this we had an intense little talk at a salon, while Cassandra played tunes without me, and not long after, we became lovers.

He was narrower in the shoulders and leaner in the torso than Collaltino had been, and he conducted himself somewhat differently in bed—he was more gradual and elaborate and more thoughtful—but what amazed me was the way desire felt the same, the way the chambers of my body flushed with the same longing and pleasure. As if all sweetness were one Sweetness, and all secrets one Secret.

Not that the details were washy to me. I had a very sharp vision of him lifting off his shirt, and later lying on the bed with his eyes closed and his mouth slack. I watched as closely as I ever had. I wanted to see the sheen of oil on the skin of his forehead, the creases at the corners of his eyes, the shadows dimming the color on the walls.

We saw each other very often that winter, and my sister said she'd never seen me get along so well with someone and complain so little. Bartolomeo had an even temperament and it took quite a lot to ruffle or annoy him. I was the one who sometimes flared up in anger when he was late or had to postpone a meeting. A hot irritation rose from my old injuries. Even then, he did not really quarrel but only looked weary. His quiet sometimes distressed me, but he was never anything but kind to me. Cassandra said that I behaved better to everyone at home, because of him.

ON EASTER SUNDAY, I woke up so heavy with sadness I had no will to move. Bartolomeo had been away with his family for two weeks and would be gone longer; he didn't know how long. I dressed myself for Mass, but I couldn't remember why I was bothering to go anywhere. I was an imprudent woman with no future. I was already near thirty, and I was going to grow old with my sister and my mother, in our little house. Bartolomeo's family, those people he was now sequestered with in the mountains, were listed in the Golden Book; their sons could serve in the Great Council and they could not marry out. There was not the smallest chance I was ever going to be a wife. Even if I were younger, even if I had a real dowry. Bartolomeo might keep me near him for decades, or he might not.

There was no reason that any of this was news to me, and my mother said I was making myself miserable for no cause. I kept myself well contained all through the service. The music of the Latin hymns made me ache for Bartolomeo, the chords made my heart solemn for him. After a while, as I sat in our pew, with the droning prayers around me and the cool-white shaft of light coming down from the dome into the darkened nave, I passed into a state without any hope at all, where hopelessness itself was a kind of comfort. I thought: *so this is the way it is,* and that phrase was beautifully clear to me. We were in church for what seemed to be a very long time, and then we went outside into the bright, bright daylight. Children were running around the square, playing and shouting. I thought I was going to be all right.

We went to eat at my uncle's house, and I let my uncle tell his same story about the fisherman's daughter and the baker's son, and I even laughed at the end. My family was relieved to see me sociable again, especially my mother.

All my delight it is, and all my joy,
To live endlessly burning, with no pain,
Not caring whether he who caused my grief
Takes pity on me.

And then Bartolomeo surprised us all by coming back early. By the end of the week he was in Venice and wanting to see me. I could not come soon enough, he said. The mountains had been very tedious without me. Nothing but clear skies and perfect vistas, what good was that to him? His spaniel barked in excitement when she heard me in the hallway, and she kept running back and forth underfoot when he and I were trying to embrace. I didn't scold him or act petulant about his being gone. It was very cozy, seeing Bartolomeo again.

And so we went on. We had our suppers in the beautifully draped little side-room, and sometimes I could hear footsteps above us or on the other side of the house; I did meet one of his brothers and a cousin, but never the females of his family. Even I knew better than to speak about this. At dinner we would have little disputes about which spices made a person more lustful and what would happen if one of us ate too much. He grew freer and more sportive as I knew him.

SOMETIMES BARTOLOMEO WAS close at hand in the evenings when I was out playing music, but he was not as eager a frequenter of salons as Collaltino had been. More than once when I walked up a stairway out into a crowded, bright room, I found myself looking for Collaltino. I looked at the backs of other men's heads, other tall blond men who had faces that were not (it always turned out) his. I was furious at him for keeping himself away. He was in some of the poems I wrote even now. I was glad, very glad, that he wasn't there. My hungers were confused, but they gnawed my heart just the same.

IN THE HOT and stifling months of summer, Bartolomeo was away from Venice on family business, a term so vague I couldn't help worrying that he had another lover. He soothed me with gifts when he came back, a necklace of garnets and a missal tooled in gold. Collaltino had given me presents too, but Bartolomeo began, as time went on, also to bring tributes to my mother and sister. Delicate and well-chosen presents, as the year passed through the calendar of feasts. We all grew used to them, a little childish under them, and used to his leaving and coming back. I had to wait each time to be summoned to him, though he could not have been more tactful in the way he handled this.

Cassandra liked Bartolomeo—she had not liked Collaltino—and she told me there was no reason that the arrangement I had with him might not be permanent. Didn't we both know a Cardinal who came to gatherings with a woman who had been his mistress for twenty years? "People live on love," she said. "Sometimes."

I said I thought the Cardinal and his mistress were living on something quite different. No matter what they said, most people knew better than to look to love if they had anything else to lean on. Only I, who had nothing else, was in its service. Only I was trying to make my home on the thinnest edge of what was possible.

I WAS ALWAYS afraid that my singing voice was going to coarsen as I got older, and I made efforts to guard against chills and currents of air that might hurt my throat. Bartolomeo used to tease me and say he was going to train his spaniel to wrap herself snugly under my chin. The first winter we were together I stayed robust and strong, and everyone said that it was because I was in good spirits, but the second winter, I was sick right after the first sleeting rain. Bartolomeo was away in Milan, and I told my family I was just as glad he didn't have to see me look ashen and clay-lipped. I lost a good deal of weight, and my mother thought she should send me to relatives in Florence, where the climate was somewhat milder.

They packed me in blankets of fur and I was ferried to the mainland and then set down in the seat of a carriage. I had not been out of my city for a long time, not since I had gone to visit Collaltino, and I tried to look out the window at the countryside and enjoy the flat valley with its sere fields and then the rising hills and the dark cypresses against the sky. I was dreamy and feverish, and a light rain fell all afternoon, followed by a lingering mist that swallowed up the hills. It seemed to me to be proof of Parmenides' notion that the world of sense is an illusion, because it consists of change. I had been reading him again, since I had the fancy that his pupil, Zeno of Elea, was the real origin of Bartolomeo's surname. In the rocking coach I did at that moment believe the world around me to be unreal. I felt myself as a very fine, still point, a dot without dimension.

My fever was worse that night at the inn, and my maid fed me spoonfuls of rice and hot milk with brandy. I slept the next day and the day after, and the rest of the trip was like falling down a long and crooked tunnel. When we got to my cousins' house, on the outskirts of Florence, I could only just sit up and speak to everyone, and I was glad to be carried into the clean, warm house that smelled of woodsmoke and heated brick.

Bartolomeo wrote me pleasant letters while I was there. "Rest the body that I love"—phrases like that. I bragged of him to my cousins. I stayed in Florence for a few months, until even my relatives agreed that I was healthy and fattened and buoyant again from their hospitality. In fact I was eager to be home with my family, where I could be more candid and less grateful.

It was early spring when I rode the ferryboat back to my city. My sister shrieked and crowed when she saw me walk through the door of the house. I said she sounded like a parrot, but I was moved by the sight of her. None of them had known just when I was returning—not Bartolomeo either, who was in the mountains for Easter. It saddened me that I couldn't see him, although I was past being tearful at waiting.

I had other friends to see, and I was busy and cheerful those first days. But later in the week I woke up with a terrible pain, somewhere under my stomach and next to my womb. I used to take herbs to ward off pregnancy, which sometimes gave me pains like this, and I thought at first that this was a ghost-pain of remembered pleasure. Whatever it was, it stayed and got worse, and by nightfall I knew that something was wrong.

My mother thought it was a spasm of heat from my old fevers, slipped down to the matrix of my body. I lay in agony for one long day and then another. Why wasn't I better, hadn't I already gotten better in Florence? None of my other illnesses had been like this, and when I moaned now I was suddenly quite angry. Where was Bartolomeo, where was Collaltino, why I was alone in this? I was not alone, my sister and my mother kept near me, but I was harsh to them and told them to go away.

"What do you want?" my sister said. "What can I bring you?"

I was flailing around beyond wants. I felt like someone in a nightmare, who'd been stabbed and couldn't get anyone to notice and take the knife out.

I sweated all night, as if I were melting. In the early hours of the morning, the room was too quiet, with Cassandra asleep in her chair by the bed. I had a great fear of dying before she woke up, but I didn't pray and I didn't ring the bell. I always thought my sister should envy me, because of the greatness of my feelings, and I still thought that, even now. I, who was so sick, thought that. I watched her soft, unweathered cheeks, moving a little with her breath, and I felt sorry for her.

The pains kept me moving—did I think I could get away from them? In the end I flung my arms above my head, as they had been placed the first time with Collaltino, and I lay like that in submission to the fevers. They were going to win. In this way I was able to be quiet and give myself over to sleep, in the time I had.

When I woke up, I felt worse. I was still very hot but my skin was dry, like the powder on a glowing coal. I could see how ill I was, but I was not afraid anymore. I always wrote of myself as *burning,* in the poems for Collaltino and Bartolomeo, and now I had the sense that I had actually set myself on fire and had been smoldering all night—I had done this terrible thing for a reason I could not fully remember but that was entirely necessary. I lay in my bed, trying to remember, and I really was quite contented.

ASHES OF LOVE

*But Nature, spent and exhausted, takes lovers back
into herself, as if there were not enough strength
to create them a second time. Have you imagined
Gaspara Stampa intensely enough so that any young girl
deserted by her beloved might be inspired
by that fierce example of soaring, objectless love
and might say to herself, "Perhaps I can be like her"?
Shouldn't this most ancient of our sufferings finally grow
more fruitful for us? Isn't it time that we lovingly
freed ourselves from the beloved and, quivering, endured:
as the arrow endures the bowstring's tension, so that
gathered in the snap of release it can be more than
itself. For there is no place where we can remain.*

—RAINER MARIA RILKE, *Duino Elegies*

I read those poems first in a hotel room in Ljubljana, in what was then Yugoslavia, not that far from where Rilke began the poems at Duino Castle outside Trieste. My girlfriend Peggy lay in bed next to me in her underwear, reading a month-old copy of *Time* magazine. People passed on printed matter in English to each other, the way they passed on coins from countries they weren't going back to or leftover bottles of antibiotics. A Canadian in our hotel gave his copy of Rilke to me. "You want this, Tom?" he said, and I gave him a sweatshirt because I thought we were leaving before we hit any cold weather. That part was a mistake. I carried *The Selected Poetry of Rainer Maria Rilke* through some pretty funky parts of Central Europe, and I read it with fervor if not always with understanding. I finally lost it years later in an airport, in a penned-in waiting area I spent too many hours in. I didn't notice until later that the book was gone, and I was too jagged to concentrate on reading anyway.

Some of the thrill I first had in reading the *Elegies* was a belief that they were truly good for me. They gave my thinking, such as it was, a shot of purer air. And yet Rilke led a fitful, neurasthenic life and behaved very badly to his wife and daughter. Not that I gave a fuck about any of that then. I was heedless and ambling and had no idea where my own honor was going to lie.

I was interested in what Rilke said about *lovers* (he was always citing them as a distinct class of people), because I was one half of a fiercely attached couple. We were in each other's sight what seemed like every minute of every day. We had screaming fights in many of the most alluring spots in the world, and once I did walk off and leave her on the beach at Split on the Dalmatian coast, when I couldn't stand to be with her one more second. But two days later at breakfast she appeared so radiantly herself to me, so intensely Peggy, that nothing could have been more essential to me than to be with her at all times.

I met Peggy in a pub in London, and when I first picked her up I thought she was hard-edged and cold. She was a pretty woman with odd features—blade-like bones and round eyes—and I didn't know how to read her expressions then. She was from Chicago, and she and her girlfriend had just been hitchhiking through France. She was surprised when I asked if anyone had given them trouble on the road. Why would they have trouble? "Little French twerps," she said. Leaning on her elbow at the bar, she listened to my stories without much apparent interest. She drank more gin than I did, and then we went back to my hotel and stayed up all night having relentless and happy sex, and we were together every day and night after that.

Maybe it was odd of us to be together like that as soon as we met. I had lived with different women through most of that decade, so it didn't seem odd to me. Peggy too had hardly been alone. Moving in with people was easy for us because we were selfish and didn't flinch at saying what we wanted and what was out of the question. Peggy was especially blunt. And I had an offhand way of being implacable.

I wasn't smitten right away. I liked Peggy fine, but it wasn't until we had been together a few weeks that the stories she told about herself began to burrow into me. How she dropped out of college to run off to Miami, how she had a biker boyfriend in high school, how her mother wouldn't send her money when she was stranded in Alabama. All this information made a nest in me. I traded back certain tales of various women I had been through love with; my life had no adventures but these. Peggy took my side in most of the incidents, even when I made a point of blaming myself.

I never thought of Peggy as a warm person—she had a distinctly sharp tongue with tram conductors and newsmen. But she was now and then suddenly tender. She'd grab my hand and kiss it while we were walking down the street, or she'd decide to slip into the tub with me in the hotel's bathroom, down the hall from our room.

Those surprises undid me. In bed I would feel a terrible mellowness in my heart. When her head was resting on my chest or we were lying flat under the covers, holding hands, I would drift off to sleep and hear myself think, *thank you for this*. Whom did I think I was thanking? There was no God I believed in at the time, but I must have been floating on reverence.

WE HAD EACH been traveling for as long as we could on as little money as we could. Our goal was to stay in London until the cash ran out, and sometimes we argued about whether tandoori takeout was too expensive or whether underground trains were a rip-off, but most of what we wanted then wasn't hard to agree on. And we had a lot of free time to spend in bed. In our poky and dismal hotel, the cleaning staff was always walking in on us. There was no time of day that the room was safe for them.

Right before we finally had to go home, we walked around in a tense glow, two people about to jump off a cloud together. We didn't even talk much about what lay ahead. Peggy's symptom here was to go steal a leather jacket for me from a very hip and expensive store on High Street Kensington. I'd always liked that store. It was a stunning gesture on her part, and it moved me greatly, despite the fact that she was caught walking out the door with the jacket in her tote bag and I had to talk the manager out of having her arrested.

Then we flew back to the States on our last dime, and settled in New York, which was my city, not hers. I got us jobs working for an antiques gallery run by people I knew. I don't know how I got us two jobs, but Peggy and I did everything together then. And they were not bad jobs either. We started off packing up the furniture that the owners took in their truck to antiques fairs all over the Atlantic seaboard, and then when I got a little more conversant with the pieces, they put me out on the floor with customers. Peggy did a lot of phone work. She could be efficient when she wanted to be, and she was good at reaching people who put her off.

Peggy liked New York (I had thought she would), and we went out almost every night, drinking and meeting people and taking the occasional drug that anyone offered, adding a needed shimmer to our days. Our days would not have made sense to us without that. One night we came out of a bar after many hours, and

I had such an expansive drunk on, I was in love with anyone who passed us on the street—how interesting and complicated they all were, what worlds of teeming detail they all contained—but I loved Peggy the most. The two of us were hanging on to each other, and I led us into the recessed doorway of an office building, where we kissed for so long that my hands moved naturally under her clothes and I wanted us to make love right then and there but I was too drunk to manage it. Peggy was laughing, the whole thing struck us as hilarious. Later, after we were back in the apartment, I lay in bed still half-dressed, with Peggy naked and asleep next to me, and I stared through a window that overlooked an air shaft, illumined by one beam of light. It was an elementary vista, and it pleased me to recognize its beauty. I felt utterly powerful, utterly at home.

WHY DID WE want to travel again, when things were good for us in New York? Well, we did want to. We talked about it quite a lot. Peggy was hungry to be all over the place, to have *place* as her occupation. She didn't want to miss anything. I too wanted to have those landscapes in me, those silhouettes on the walls of my psyche. And I still think: even when you can't wait to get out of some hellhole you've chosen to visit, later you're never sorry you were there.

It wasn't that hard then to save some money up, if you had a cheap apartment. So we worked for a year and we went back to Europe, to Rome this time and up to Venice and then down the other side of the Adriatic to Split and from Dubrovnik by boat over to Corfu. We stopped when we got to Turkey, and Peggy complained because we didn't have the money to go farther into Asia, now that we were at its threshold. She was a good traveler because she was fearless, and a bad one because she could take an instant dislike to a place if it displeased her right away. I was more curious, better at picking up languages and bits of handy information, but I was the one who had harebrained schemes for getting to unreachable spots.

Peggy was good at making observations. She said, "No one has ever actually said *excuse me* in Serbo-Croatian" and "The light in Greece makes travelers believe they're intelligent." These were not often wrong, but she was a conceited traveler—her own remarks were all she needed from a place. I had other needs. I wanted to be changed forever by what I took in, a voyager returned with visionary glints in his eyes. But what I was going to do with myself then? I must have pictured my later self as rich in something I couldn't spend.

We had fine times in Turkey, but getting back was less fun. Peggy was crabby about having to go by bus all the way back through Central Europe. In Zagreb, where we stopped overnight, she got into a quarrel with a man who was selling cheese at a marketplace. Peggy was bargaining for the cheese by letting the man write down numbers—usually a good-humored process—but here she thought the man was mocking her. She thought he drew the *8* as the figure of a nude woman and the *9* as a penis. She shouted to me to witness his drawing. The numerals looked ordinary to me, penciled in European script on a paper bag. The man did laugh meanly once he saw she was not going to buy anything.

"He's a scumbag," she said. Fortunately this word was outside whatever English he had. When I told her to keep her voice down, she turned and darted away from me. Where did she go? I lost sight of her at once. I walked through every boulevard and alley in that part of the city, for hours and hours. It was a handsome city, rich in stately Baroque hulks and Gothic churches with painted tile roofs and medieval stone gates, but I didn't care about any of it then.

At the end of the afternoon I suddenly saw her—Peggy herself, drinking a glass of canned plum juice at a streetside counter. "The man was a thief," she said, but I knew she was glad to see me.

I did not admire Peggy when she acted this way. Suspicion, scorn, hotheadedness about money: these were not traits I admired. I had left other women over behavior much more subtle than this. But I saw that I didn't care when Peggy was dead wrong. My feelings for her were independent of any opinion. They ran in a different channel, they had their own route. It was an odd, heady sensation to know this. I kissed her neck, in full sincerity.

She was queenly under my kisses. "Get me out of this country," she said.

"I'm working on it," I said.

Afterward she referred to this as the time we faced down those Croats, and that may have been how she really remembered it.

———

AND THERE WERE beautiful things in that part of the world too. From the bus on the highway, in Slovenia, we saw a man in a cart driving an ox to plow his field. The field was surrounded by deep hills—dry dirt bordered by high grasses—and the ox was solid brown, a lumbering creature intent on his task. It seemed miraculous to me that the ox was moving matter-of-factly across the landscape, an action so ancient. The man worked alone, in a dirt-smeared shirt and workpants, his face hidden by a cap. Peggy and I watched for as long as he and the yoked ox remained in sight. There were unplowed hills all around, slopes of scrub-brush and gnarled trees. The field seemed to be in the middle of nowhere. Where was the man's house? Where was his barn, the rest of his farm? It was all unknowable. I was taking it in, nonetheless.

What did I think I was doing with this ox, this hoarded experience? I was spinning matter into thought, making a cocoon I could carry with me. Nothing seemed more necessary. Peggy and I held hands, after the ox had passed.

It is always hard to explain to people what I actually *did* all day when I was traveling. And would I have gone so many places if I'd never met Peggy? Probably not. It was an appetite we acted out together. Parts of every trip were disappointing and humiliating. Parts were so full of our own stupidities that they could not be talked about at all later on. This did not curb our zeal. We came home and worked, oh, for a year or so, always with the idea that we were about to leave sometime soon. It seemed that our task was to go and view extraordinary things—we told people we were going to "go take a look."

PEGGY MUST HAVE gotten pregnant when we were in Bangkok, on a night after we'd been fighting. It had been Peggy's idea to see more of Asia, but I liked Thailand better than she did. We had trouble keeping expenses down when we first got there, cheap though everything was. One morning we had a pointless argument about who smoked more cigarettes and wasted money on them, and she went off without me. "Just let me do what I *want*," she said. "Is that too much to ask?"

I lay in bed, slowly eating a rose-apple I had bought the day before and reading Rilke's poems.

> *And yet, when you have survived*
> *the terror of the first glances, the longing at the window,*
> *and the first walk together, only once, through the garden:*
> *lovers,* are *you the same? When you lift yourselves up*
> *to each other's mouth and your lips join, drink against drink:*
> *oh how strangely each drinker seeps away from his action.*

I got up then and walked around the city. I wasn't used to seeing any place without Peggy, although I should have been glad to be without her. The air, for all its industrial smells, felt balmy and soft. But there were too many people, why were there so many people? Just for a taste of quiet, I slipped into a walled court, a

green and palmy spot, where I walked around a temple compound and stood for a while looking at yet another statue of the
Buddha.

It was an especially exquisite statue. The figure was entirely
gold, and his head was framed by the pointed arch of a flame, a
flame that meant both the passions burning out and the blaze of
enlightenment. Around me people were coming and going, as
they did in Thai temples, lighting incense sticks and setting
down intricate necklaces of flowers in front of different altars. It
was just before noon, the monks' last meal of the day.

What's the point of eating so seldom? I thought, and the question was a knot I carried with me for the rest of the day, all
through my own delicious lunch of catfish over rice from a curry
shop and the snack of fried peanut cookies I had later on with
Guy, a Californian from our hotel whom I ran into on the street.
Are they in this world or not, those skinny monks? What do they
think they're doing?

Guy said, "Are you planning to become a monk?"

"All these young Thai men do it," I said. "They take vows and
then they come back out again after a few months. It's very
usual."

"I know," Guy said. "It's an interesting country."

"The country's full of people who've done time as monks the
way other people go into the army. I've never heard of such a
thing anywhere."

"Personally," he said, "I think you should move here. It suits
you."

It was just a passing remark, but I was enormously flattered that anyone would say such a thing. I walked home through the thronged and noisy streets, through this city that always felt like a future too dense to be lived in, and I was high as a kite on my sudden affinity for the place. The neon signs in Thai and the dinky motorcycle taxis that sounded like buzz saws and the sudden glimpse of boats on the canals all struck me with an owner's rapture. I was in the right part of the world.

When I came back to our room in the guest house, there were two sky-blue packs of Gauloises on the pillow, which Peggy had left as a peace offering to me. She had put an orchid blossom, magenta centered with white, next to these, so that the colors leaped against each other in the light. Peggy herself was lying with her head on the other pillow, her short hair in childish tufts and her eyes just opening as I came in. So much is given to me, I thought.

She seemed happy to see me, relieved that I wasn't holding a grudge as I sometimes did. When I lay down next to her and we turned toward each other on the bed, my craving for her came up from very deep in me, so that the peak of arousal was close to heartbreak.

IF THAT WAS when our son was conceived, we didn't know for a while. We were distracted by a number of things—what happened to our luggage in Chumphon and why we couldn't find the right hotel in Hat Yai. On the bus ride down the Malay peninsulas we disagreed about whether the country of Thailand was being ruined by capitalist greed (Peggy said yes, I said that was a simplistic idea), and we got too annoyed to be able to look into each other's faces for the whole ride. Peggy gazed out the window and I read my books, although the scenery was spectacular. Green rice paddies, distant hills, thick rainforest, shining rivers. When I bothered to look up, I was enchanted.

If only we too could discover a pure, contained
human place, our own strip of fruit-bearing soil
between river and rock. For our own heart always exceeds us.

I was reading Rilke on the bus. Peggy slept a lot. The bus was an open-sided truck with rows of seats and it stopped at every town along the way.

At one stop an English-speaking couple got on, and I was thrilled to have people to talk to. But I thought Peggy paid too much attention to the husband from Brisbane. "I can't even *flirt,*" she said to me later. "You can't stand even a basic human activity like that."

"You *can't* flirt," I said. "There's no distance between flirting and fucking for you."

We left them outside Penang, but the Australian husband did send Peggy a postcard in the U.S. some time later. Remember me? it said. Our paths could cross again. I hope.

The monsoon season started while we were on a different bus. Out the window (this bus had windows) sheets of rain fell and afterward a steamy vapor rose from the land. Peggy didn't exactly know when she'd had her last period, but she thought the delay was just from the rigors of traveling and from not eating as well as she should have been. Certain realities were not very vivid to us to then. It wasn't until we came back to the States that we knew, and she was into her fourth month by then. So we had to go with it. Perhaps that was what we both wanted to do anyway.

We are not in harmony, our blood does not forewarn us
like migratory birds'. Late, overtaken,
we force ourselves abruptly onto the wind
and fall to earth at some iced-over lake.

How could I not have known? We slept naked next to each other every night, we talked about our every digestive upheaval and bug bite. I kept close to anything Peggy did, even when we quarreled. What biosphere were we living in? The sack of our *feelings,* the pocket of our "relationship." All that emotion, and we forgot about the rules of nature.

What would I have said to her if I had known for certain earlier on that she was carrying a child? Don't do it, Peggy. You'll lose your footing, you'll slip and fall and reap havoc. You'll be sorry.

I wouldn't have said that. I loved Peggy. I was excited, in a blurred sort of way, about being a father. I didn't have the skill to look too far ahead. People seemed glad they had kids, and I had all I could do to get used to the idea. I was a man, so it was still an idea to me. Part of me probably thought that Peggy had made it up.

Peggy was pretty volatile during her pregnancy. Sometimes she gloated and bragged and was ethereally smug. "A pregnant woman," she'd say, "can see right through people." And sometimes she referred to herself as knocked up and went back to smoking cigarettes. "Will you put that *out?*" I'd say, but we were too young to truly worry about safety.

And we were right. The birth, although it was harrowing to both of us, was in fact very straightforward, we were told. I was white with fright at the spectacle of Peggy doing something so unlike her, submitting to round after round of torment for an outcome she had not even asked for. The heroics forced on her astounded me. Peggy herself cursed through most of it. "Don't fucking tell me what to do," she said to the doctor.

She was subdued and chastened by the time we brought the baby home, as if the three days in the hospital had involved more punishing shocks. My son Eli was a lump of flesh wrapped in white flannel, a wailing and wriggling biped with features just starting to be human. I loved him from the first, but I could not believe they were leaving us alone with him.

Peggy saw his spirit, I have to give her that. In those early days, when he was just a dainty blob of protoplasm to me, I would hear her talk to the baby. "You hear me, sweetie," she would say to him. "Little sharp-ears. You know what's what."

I could list the times when I felt closest to Peggy: the first weeks together in the hotel bed in London; certain moments when we were traveling; and the early days when Eli was a new baby. This last phase, with its broken nights and hazy mornings, was unmixed with sex. I was swept up in another amazement, but it confused me to be with Peggy with no desire acted out between us. I waited for her through those months—I wasn't an oaf or a boor or a brute—but my existence, even with the baby in it, seemed less real to me.

I hadn't really been without contact with a female body since I was a teenager, not for more than a few weeks at a time. My whole life had been bound up with women. I fell in love with them and lived with them. I didn't see how people led any other sort of life.

I wasn't used to being at work without Peggy around, and I hated being away all day. I'd call and wake her from her naps. But Eli was thriving. "Little fat boy," Peggy said. "You take nourishment from the air, you feed on everyone's vibrations." The doctor said he was gaining at a very good rate. When I carried him in his pouch across my chest, I could feel his weight pulling sweetly at my shoulders. I was proud of us.

I had never expected Peggy to be such a confident mother. "Worry less, please," she told me. I was the one who thought the baby shouldn't go outside without a cap and shouldn't play on the dirty wooden floors of our apartment. Peggy would dangle him upside down by his feet (he laughed), she would hold him in the crook of her arm while she carried a pot of hot soup in her other hand. "Relax," she would say to me.

And Peggy, who had always been bony and slim, now had lush breasts, a slacker figure. At the end of six months, when she came to me again as a lover, I felt newly held and enveloped, settled *in the bosom of my family,* where I was a contented man. I had been so idle and young before this, and now the world had come to claim me.

We had a few different babysitters—a fuchsia-haired girl from the neighborhood, a nursing student, a gay guy in his thirties. They all seemed fine to us. But I shouldn't have left Peggy alone so much. I should have just quit my stupid job, people think jobs are everything. The antiques place I worked in was written up in the Home section of the *Times,* and all of a sudden we were swamped with calls from decorators. I was on the phone for hours, answering questions from the most meticulous people in the world, and I had to stay late night after night. I missed Eli. When a woman with a client from Southampton canceled a lunch we were supposed to have, I ran home to steal a break with my son.

I heard him crying from the hallway. He could set up a good yowl when he wanted to. "Hey, guy, I know how you feel," I said, as I came through the door. "It's me, Peg. I'll walk him around."

Peggy didn't answer. The baby was standing up in his crib, holding on to the railing and belting out his complaints. "Eli the man," I said. "I'm here." I lifted him up and patted his back while he wailed. I thought Peggy must be in the bathroom or on the phone. She wasn't. She wasn't anywhere. The baby's diaper needed replacement, and I changed it, which I thought was a nice thing for me to do before she got back from wherever she was. He didn't like being changed, in his current mood, and he did a lot of kicking. I walked him through every corner of our small apartment, expecting Peggy to emerge from some hidden nook. Or one of the sitters, although it wasn't their time. Eli was still crying, but more softly, when I sat down on the sofa with him and waited. I waited and waited, getting angrier every second. I fed him a bottle. I put him in his crib. I waited for two hours, and then I heard a key in the lock, and Peggy came through the door and gave a small shriek when she saw me.

The baby was sleeping, so I didn't want to shout. "You *left* him?" I said. "You left Eli this long?"

"He was fine," Peggy said. "People think babies can't be alone but they can be."

"What?" I said. "What did you say?"

"Eli never does anything stupid. He knows I'm coming home."

"Never?" I said. My head was cracking from inside.

"Just tell me," I said. "You can tell me. You leave him like this all the time?"

"He's fine," Peggy said. "He's always been fine."

Her eyes were tight and ashamed, but her mouth was petulant. "I didn't bother to tell you," she said, "because I knew how you would be about it. And look."

"Where did you go?" I said.

"Nowhere," she said. "Just around."

I did shout then, and I woke my son. I kept asking Peggy, what was the matter with her, what did she think she was doing? I followed her around, bellowing, fighting for an answer, which I did believe was my right. Peggy took the baby from his crib and soothed him and looked at me irately.

I shouted at her for days. There was a piece of her missing, I thought. I made her cry, with my bullying, but she was only crying in pity for herself at having a mate like me. Nothing had happened to Eli, why should she feel remorse?

What about when Eli got big enough to climb out of his crib? "He won't do that," Peggy said. "He's very sensible." *She's at her wit's end,* I thought, *and she doesn't know it.* I was afraid to leave her alone for too long with Eli, despite her promises, those vows made only to humor me. I borrowed money and had Manny, our favorite sitter, come in more often. I sent friends over to be with her. I left work early as often as I could, oftener.

Who was this woman? She looked like the ruin of someone I loved. Ropy and tired and tight around the mouth. The beautiful ruin. I loved her. When I came home, I would hold her to my chest and kiss the top of her head, the way I kissed the baby's head. It made her smile. There was still a taste of floating lust between us, but whatever happened in bed did not do us much good. Who was she?

I CAME HOME one night with cartons of Chinese food for supper, and there was no one in the house. It was a cool fall day, and if Peg and Eli were lingering in the park, I hoped she had put enough clothes on him. Or she might have gone to visit one of her friends. It occurred to me, not for the first time, that she had a lover.

After I got sick of waiting, I heated up some of the food for myself, and when I sat down at the table, I saw her note for me on the pad where we kept shopping lists.

We're gone—I'll call. Eli is fine.

What did it mean? I knew what it meant. Peggy had left me and taken Eli. She had gone to someone—she would never do anything like this alone—and I had no idea who the man was, which seemed particularly bitter to me. I had nothing to do with any of this. Nothing was mine.

I stood up, since it was clear I had to do something. When I tore the note off the pad, my hands were shaking with anger. In a movie, an actor playing me might have thrown pieces of furniture around the room. The chairs, the table, the high chair. I had the feeling that there was such a movie playing somewhere, while I stood perfectly still, and fury went through me like a jolt of current. I knew that if I went into the bedroom, I would see the empty spaces in the blue-painted cubby where Eli's things were kept, and I didn't want to go in there. I sat down again at the kitchen table and waited for Peggy to telephone me.

IF SHE HADN'T sounded so pleased with herself, maybe we could have worked it out right then. "Peggy," I said. "You can't do it this way. You just can't."

"This is my way. This is the way I do it."

She was sorry, she said, but her leaving was for the best. "For the best"—she'd never used a prissy phrase like that in her life. Whose language was this?

"This was a very hard thing to do," she said.

Did she want compliments on her bravery? From me?

"Can you listen for a minute?" she said. "Is that too much to ask? We couldn't go on the way we were."

"Why not?" I said. "Why not?"

"There was nothing there," she said.

And then I did shout every single thing I could at her, every mistake of hers I could jeer at, every intimate secret I could point to in wild disgust. And who was this Richard? Oh, not anyone I knew. He was a lawyer. A what? Well, not exactly a lawyer. He had left law school and he had his own business. What business? A laundromat. A laundromat! Mr. Clean Machine. Mr. Suds, Esquire. I couldn't stop when I heard that.

THROUGHOUT THE first year there were times when we might have gotten back together. We would snarl and rage, and then a spark of our old affection would make us sentimental again. Every week she brought Eli to see me, and sometimes she simply dropped him off and fled, and sometimes we both played with him, dancing him around or doing funny voices for his toys. I tickled Eli and then I tickled Peggy too, Eli cackled and crowed, the three of us snuggled together in the bed. Then Eli would get wild and speedy, and Peggy would announce that I was bad for him. "Maybe we shouldn't come anymore," she'd say. Eli would cry. Peggy would say, "He's better with Richard." "You're not much of a mother," I'd say. In short, we made a mess of things. We made everything worse.

I kept away from Richard, who seemed slick and crazy to me. Why had Peggy picked him? Every week, after Peggy took Eli back, I'd feel like shooting myself or shooting her. After we had gone on like this for almost a year, I did something I should never have done. I left New York. I moved to California, where my family was. I kept calling Eli on the phone every few days but he wasn't even two years old yet, he had no real idea where I was.

I stayed in Mill Valley, at my cousin's, in a room over his garage. I woke up each day desperate with loneliness. I walked around like a zombie of grief. I was looking for work, but in the first weeks I had nothing to distract me from the mortal agony of missing what I'd once had. Every night I had supper with my cousin Aaron and his wife and two kids—they were very nice to me—and then I'd lie in bed in my room over the garage, with its dusty shag carpeting and its smell of mice, and I would think, *how did it get this way?* I couldn't bear not seeing Eli, and I was homesick for what Peggy had been to me. That I had taken myself to the other side of the continent did not keep me from the torment of waiting for her in vain, like any abandoned lover.

But Nature, spent and exhausted, takes lovers back
into herself, as if there were not enough strength
to create them a second time. Have you imagined
Gaspara Stampa intensely enough so that any young girl
deserted by her beloved might be inspired
by that fierce example of soaring, objectless love
and might say to herself, "Perhaps I can be like her"?
Shouldn't this most ancient of our sufferings finally grow
more fruitful for us?

I had to buy a new Rilke because I had lost the other copy at the airport in Singapore. I still thought that Peggy would come back to me. Maybe she thought so too. Before I left, I had been giving her money from time to time, and I sent her some from California, after I got work refinishing oak chests and tables for a vintage furniture dealer nearby. Not a lot of money, but some for the baby. I called her to make sure she got it, just to hear her thank me.

Sometimes when I called New York to check on Eli, I'd start fighting with Peggy again, fighting and then pleading. The old accusations, the old imploring. "It's not too late. Why do you think it's too late?" I said. "Are you listening?" The phone was in my cousin's kitchen and the family heard me from the living room, embarrassed for me and puzzled. I knew better than to hope for anything from Peggy. This did not keep me from wanting her.

I HAD TO remember how many other people had been morons the way that I was being one now. There wasn't much other consolation available. Lying in bed back in my cruddy room over the garage, I imagined Gaspara Stampa, as Rilke suggested. A note in another book told me that she was a poet (1523–1554) of unhappy love sonnets (two hundred forty-five on that one unending subject). She was still read quite widely in Italy. Even before Rilke wrote the *Elegies*, he had made the narrator of *Malte Laurids Brigge* say, "Women like Stampa hurl themselves after the man they have lost, but with the first steps they overtake him, and in front of them is only God."

I didn't feel that God was in front of me, but I began to want something like Him to be. The ideas I'd lived on weren't strong enough for this next stretch, I could see that. Nothing I knew was much help to me now. As a young man, all my longings had been around sex—when did I have occasion to think of anything else? Now I lived in that occasion. In Rome I had seen a mosaic in the Basilica di San Clemente of a deer dipping its nose in a blue stream, symbol of the soul's thirst for God.

My cousins talked me into going with them to Friday night services at their very liberal synagogue, but the prayers (even the familiar ones) didn't stir me and certainly didn't comfort me. The liturgy filled my mind with objections to it. I only went that once.

I was friends with Gary, the antiques dealer I worked for, and he took me a few times to his Buddhist meditation group—I had the idea that I knew something about this, since I'd been to Thailand, but I didn't, not at all. I didn't much like it either. Sitting there only made me think of Peggy. It was especially bad for me toward the end of the forty-five-minute sit, when my mind could not keep from picking over its wounds. I was thrilled when someone rang the little gong that meant the sitting part was over. I'd go home and think, *nothing's going to fucking help.*

I worked hard at the job for Gary—that was how I kept from going under altogether. I learned from him whatever he knew about the pieces we were handling, the armoires and vases and Hoosier cabinets and once a potbellied stove from 1875, the year

(I remembered) of Rilke's birth. We had everything from formica to Mission Oak to ivory. "Between junk and glory" was our slogan. "Think of us as plucking lotuses out of the muck," Gary said.

I enjoyed looking at objects closely. It reminded me of traveling, of the days spent gazing and walking around to get a better view. I was only fair as a furniture refinisher, but my opinions about what pieces to buy were good and got better. Sellers and buyers trusted me because I was low-key, and I didn't cheat them, but I was wily in my way. It was a small business, and I rose from handyman to partner in about a minute. I had time to read in the field, books and trade publications and magazines, and I had a sense of what people were going to want next. Shutting up is a good research tool.

For a while I lived in the back of Gary's house, and I liked to go out to the shed to look over the stored objects, to poke and examine and ponder. Gary used to say I was like a farmer checking on his sheep. I came to know certain pieces very well— a painted bench from Mexico that was much too big for its purpose, a bamboo dressing table from the thirties, a stenciled stoneware crock from Illinois that pickles had been stored in. I liked identifying the marks of human use, the scuffs and hollows, the smoke stains and ink smudges.

Often when Gary and I were selling a piece, we would tell people something like, "What parties this punch bowl has seen!" I was aware always of the irony there—I who was so taken with the amount of *feeling* left in these objects hardly lived in the outside world at all. No quaffing any punch to the last drop for me.

But I'd done my quaffing, hadn't I? Mostly I seemed to be finished and spent. I found myself on the other side of things, which turned out to be a realm with its own scenery. Sometimes what I had was quite beautifully sufficient.

And the external
shrinks into less and less. Where once an enduring house was,
now a cerebral structure crosses our path . . .

I leaned on Rilke quite a lot at this time.

I MIGHT HAVE gone on like this, flourishing ever more fully in the space of my own head. I was making my way to something, slowly. But when Eli was five, Peggy decided that he should come to live with me.

"It's time," she said, in a solemn voice that bugged me. I think Peggy was not in good shape—she and Richard the Suds had split up, and she had been living at a bunch of different phone numbers, crashing with friends or staying with various guys. She wanted to go back to London—she said she needed a change—but she wouldn't say how long she had in mind. "Eli will be fine with this," she said.

I had not seen Eli since he was a baby. I was always planning to go back East to see him, but I didn't. In our phone talks, I would get him to narrate what he'd been doing, and I had my goofy questions I'd been teasing him with for years, but you couldn't say we had a smooth back-and-forth. A delight with a huge amount of panic in it rose in me at this news.

I knew what he looked like in his pictures—a stringy little boy with dark hair and pale skin. But I didn't really know a thing. In the weeks before he arrived, I stayed by myself as much as I possibly could. I was renting a bungalow at the end of a gravel road, and I sat outside under the eucalyptus trees in the yard, inhaling their medicinal scent and looking at the blue western sky. I was trying to savor my last days of inwardness. There was an iridescent glass vase from the twenties that I was deciding about (unsigned but maybe a Loetz), and I held it in the sunlight to study its shimmering tints and to check for nicks. I wasn't going to be keeping anything fragile in the house anymore, was I?

IT WAS NOT Peggy who brought Eli to me but her mother, who traveled from Chicago to New York to fetch him and then all the way to me in California. Rita was a nervous and silly woman, but she'd always liked me and she waved madly when they walked through the gate at the airport. "Look at this boy!" she said, holding Eli's hand. Eli seemed dazed, as well he might, but he looked so *actual* to me I could hardly stand it—his skin too fresh and delicate, his mouth too mobile, his eyes too glinting. I was beside myself. "Hi, boy," I said.

Eli did not talk much that first day. Rita and I were hearty and brisk around him—"Here we are!" "You ate your whole lunch!" "You have a yard now!"—and he watched us. When Rita left in the evening, she said, "Be good, pumpkin."

He said, "I'm *not* a vegetable," with a little smirk. He didn't seem upset at her going, but she wasn't someone he knew very well.

"You know what I like to do?" he said to me while we were standing outside in the twilight. "Guess."

"Wrestle alligators?"

"Nope."

"Jump tall buildings at a single bound?"

"*No.*"

"End world hunger?"

"I like to listen to the radio before I go to bed."

"No problem," I said.

"That's what you think," he said.

What he liked, I discovered when he fooled with the tuning dial, was hip-hop music played very loud. He did actually fall asleep with it blaring, with the rhyming engine of the lines going on and on. I was so happy that he was sleeping soundly in my house that I left the radio on for an hour, although it drove me nuts and made me feel old.

Noise was his element, it turned out. On good days, he was excited and shrieking. On bad days, he was sullen and explosive. I had once heard a comedian say that living with kids is like having a bowling alley installed in your brain, and I quoted that line to anyone who asked. Eli needed (as Peggy advised me from London) a lot of stimulation. He was at his worst—lonely for his mother, angry over the move, hostile to me—when there was nothing buzzing or banging or bleating in front of him. Well. If that was what it took. He was a great boy, under all that crashing noise, funny and full of ideas and very smart. I had to think of places to take him—parks and roller rinks and swimming pools. I had to keep him moving; I had to be on the case every second, in the early days. Once he got used to me, he was a snuggler too, but that didn't happen for a while.

AT FIRST, Peggy phoned us often—at seven in the morning, U.S. time. For a while there was talk of her coming back to take Eli to London, and then that idea petered out, before I even argued with her. I got his musical taste expanded to samba, John Philip Sousa, and the Sex Pistols, which may not have been an improvement. He played around in the backyard with another boy from school—they threw rocks into the compost heap, they pretended to be space aliens, I don't know what they did. He liked the yard.

But sometime during that year, Eli began to know that Peggy wasn't coming back for him anytime soon, and California suddenly soured for him. He hated the way everything *looked,* he thought all the people were *stupid.* He called everyone in his class a shithead, he threw a toy truck at a girl's chest. His school complained. When I spoke to him, he turned his back. He had come through the first months so well, and now I was afraid he was going to turn into a kid I couldn't handle. This was a very bad time.

A WOMAN CAME into the store one day to buy a dresser and she flirted with me. I was astonished. She was distinctly pretty, leaning toward me in a skimpy T-shirt, a small blond person who asked a lot of questions and then asked me how I knew all that. I couldn't get over it. I was like an innocent yokel with his mouth wide open, although I hadn't been altogether celibate during these years. But she arrived just when I was thinking that nothing, nothing, was ever easy in my life—why wasn't it? why not?—and here she was, so mild and good-looking and interested.

She asked me if some long wooden hairpins with carved tops were Chinese, which they were.

"We had one like that on the knickknack shelf in our house," she said. "My great-great-grandmother sent it back. She was a missionary in China. Well, a missionary's wife."

"The missionaries were very tough," I said. "Very sturdy types." I made that up, what did I know about it? I was just talking. I invited her back to the house for dinner the same day.

Eli said, "Who's this dweeb?" when she walked in, but I had more or less warned her and she laughed him off. Her name was Mattina, and Eli kept singing over and over the refrain from "Frère Jacques," "Sonny lemon tina! Sonny lemon tina! Ding dang dong! Ding dang dong!" She was a good sport about everything. We had to talk loudly over his video cartoons, as if we were in some comedy about the dating dad. Actually, this chore of voicing breathy sentences into each other's ear began to feel quite sexy. She was so round and smooth and calm about herself, just waiting for me to figure out how to get us into bed, with Eli right there in the next room. She was younger than I was, somewhere in her mid-twenties, and I could see that for her nothing was very difficult yet.

I shamelessly let Eli watch a cop show on TV that I usually banned, and while he was hynotized by the tube, I snuck her off into the yard for some heavy petting. She was a graceful kisser, unflustered by any awkwardness, sleepy-eyed and friendly. She laughed softly when I took off her bra.

ELI WAS NOT crazy about her. At the time they met, he didn't care for anyone—man, woman, dog, cat—but even later he didn't seem to get past a certain point with Mattina, though they got along all right. But I saw my chance and I took it. I saw that I could have a less starved and cramped and insane existence. Mattina was a day at the beach, a walk in the park, a piece of cake. And not stupid. She worked in a lab at Berkeley, helping some big-deal botanist with his hybrids. She was probably smarter than I was.

And what did she want with me, a gloomy guy with a screeching imp of a son? I don't think she knew any better—she might have fallen into any attraction that offered, and I was older and seemed glamorous to her. I needed her very badly. We had a good time together, quite often. I wasn't in love with her exactly, not in the way I had been when I was younger, but she was such a pleasant, fair-minded person—it awed me sometimes. I was *moved to appreciation*. It is hard to explain how moving that can be.

Once Eli knew Mattina was coming to live with us, he said,

"Are we getting a swimming pool too?" When he was that little, I couldn't always tell if he was making a joke, but I knew he was linking Mattina to something like bourgeois comfort, a less slipshod lifestyle. No more Fritos for breakfast, no more going to school in his pajama top. There would be trips to the mall, rides to baseball games.

All Mattina asked was that I not condescend to her for being young (as I sometimes did) and that I make room for her in the household as my cherished consort. She complained when I could never remember what days she worked at the lab, but she was ridiculously touched when I brought home a quart of the ice cream she liked. It made no sense that this terrific-looking young woman had to fight for my attention, but that was the premise we lived under. She cajoled and bribed and gently bullied me. Gary said I was a lucky jerk.

And so I was thrown back once again into the mundane world of human relations. There was my wild-guy-Eli making his many decibels of noise that had to be dealt with, and there was Mattina with her sweetness and caresses and her friends who liked to visit. My days did not have a second of solitude in them. I was in the thick of some kind of talk-talk-talk in every waking hour. Gone was my long spell of silent study and inner ripening. Vanished without a trace.

Rilke—I knew from my reading—never saw his daughter Ruth very much after her first year. She was left as an infant with his wife Clara's parents in the country, and Rilke lived intermittently with his wife, a sculptor, for just a little while longer, and then he slipped away from the confinement of those bonds. He was always shaking off women. One after another. I didn't want to be like Rilke. I was ashamed for both of us. I just wanted Eli to be all right, I wanted to build a nest that could safely hold him.

Eli had been sleeping on a daybed in the study, and Mattina made me set up a real room for him. She took him to the mall to get Batman sheets and a red plaid quilt and a lot of other crap. He was cosseted with toys and given books he couldn't read yet and fitted with overpriced running shoes. This distracted him from being impossible. He didn't mean to improve but he did, in fits and starts.

From England, Peggy made a few snotty remarks about how much money I seemed to have now—where had it been before?—but she wasn't as annoying as she might have been. This decision of hers to be relatively agreeable meant, I thought, that she was expecting Eli to stay with me longer. "His feet will grow out of those fancy sneakers overnight," she said. "You'll see."

Right away I had the idea (we all did, from our own angles) that if I married Mattina, I had a stronger case for keeping Eli with me. It wasn't a legal question—Peggy and I never went to law, and who knows what rights I would have had—but I thought the gesture would make a lasting impression on Peggy. This was probably right.

Mattina and I had a wedding in our yard, with amazing flowers provided by her cronies from work and many bottles of champagne drunk by cute young women and perfectly nice young men I didn't especially want to talk to. I was a tense, somewhat embarrassed groom, and nobody thought this was odd. Mattina looked excited and pretty, in a little short white sheath. My family liked her. Gary and his boyfriend paid to have someone play the flute for us in our driveway. From across the ocean, Peggy made fun of our not having a honeymoon, but she sent a silk bowtie for Eli to wear.

Later Peggy and I had disputes about his upbringing, and when Eli was older he went to spend summers with her in England, but my marriage did help bind him to me. In our wedding pictures Eli looks toothy and pleased. And it would have been much, much harder to raise him without Mattina. I can't even think how it would have been.

PEOPLE KNOW WHEN you're not in love with them. It can be kept a secret for only so long. For the first five years Mattina chose to assume that I was just older, more tempered and moderate than other men she'd known. Or that I wasn't open about my emotions, as many American men weren't. I did try to be kind to her. The kindness and the tender adventures of lust kept us going for a long time.

At one point Mattina started to think that I had a lover, when I was out at night too much. I was really with Gary's Vipassana meditation group, which I had decided to try again. I didn't know how to make Mattina believe that was really where I was, and the quarrel we had about it, in which she cited all the ways I didn't notice her, broke open more pockets of sadness from her than I'd known about. "I notice you all the time," I said, and then I argued that couples never stayed in their first full delirious flush forever anyway, how could they? "You were never in any flush," she said.

I did get her to believe that I was where I said I was on those Thursday evenings, just sitting still and trying to focus on my breath. "Why your breath?" she said. "It's handy," I said. "It's something I can observe without fear or clinging." After that she accused me of going out every week to learn not to feel, a thing I was already good at. But she did believe me.

At this point in my life, I took to it pretty readily—the meditation, the discussions afterward, the whole package. I was often sleepy and distracted and completely unable to concentrate, but I was in thrall to the notion of going beyond my own particulars.

Eli, who was almost eleven when I started this, kind of liked my having this new hobby, which he connected with his favorite kung-fu movies, despite my disclaimers. "Sorry to tell you it doesn't involve kicking people," I said. And even Mattina got used to it, when she saw that I wasn't going to leave her, that I was going to do everything else the way I'd always done it. She did want me to be happy, after all.

IT WASN'T UNTIL Eli was in his early teenagehood and he flew across the ocean by himself to spend a month with his mother in England, that I decided what I needed was to go off alone for a week to Yosemite. Not to meditate—I had already hit

my limits with that—but just to hang out by myself, in a landscape of noble heights and thrilling chasms, with no one talking
to me all the time, no one. Mattina was disappointed that this
was my idea of a blissful vacation. But it wasn't an eccentric thing
to do in California, and she didn't try to block me.

So I took off in the car with my backpack and a new tent, and
I picked the trails I thought were the least popular, although of
course there were other humans often within sight. I got sprayed
on by spectacular waterfalls, and I saw a Sequoia that was thirty
feet thick, and I passed through meadows ringed by granite
peaks. One afternoon I sat for an hour looking at the rock walls
of Half Dome, and I remembered myself in a place like Prague,
gazing at the tower of St. Vitus Cathedral. But when I was young
I took things in differently. I thought I was giving them their
meaning by dowering them with my attention. What did I know
then of what else would be asked of me? I didn't know how life
would shout at me and tug my arm and bellow commands. I'd
had another idea completely.

The whole week I got rained on only once, a pelting thunder-
storm that was over fast. And when I came back from Yosemite,
after not speaking to another person for a week, tired and
unbathed and rank-smelling, I was more changed than I'd
expected. It was not that I was calmer (everyone's idea of why I'd
gone), but that the world seemed newly proportioned, as if I had
judged the relative size of its parts wrong before now.

When I hugged Mattina to me, I couldn't get over the delicate
sturdiness of her. How delicious the pressure of her hug was. I

was spacey when I first got back, but not hard to get along with. "Just don't feed me any freeze-dried chili," I said. "I missed your beautiful food, girl." I wanted to be nicer to her.

My visual sense was especially sharp—the roses Mattina had planted in the yard were a startling creamy-peach color, vibrant and lush. Not talking for so long had a good aftereffect. In the shop, objects displayed their details to me in a single glimpse. Under this spell of acuteness, I found a hairline crack in a creamware plate that Gary was going to buy, so we paid a lower price for it, although it seemed laughable to me that people cared about cracks, as if the world weren't naturally cracking and dissolving every second anyway.

ELI CAME BACK from England that summer with a duffel bag full of unbelievably raucous CDs. Thick, anarchic blasts of roiling rock 'n' roll. Peggy had let him go off on his own quite a lot, and he was proud of this, ready to continue being more independent of pesky adults. He liked to call Mattina "Fat-Tina"—in fact, she was still slender and sexy—but otherwise he wasn't a hostile, horrible teenager, comparatively speaking. But after this summer he was away from the house all the time—on his own, with his friends, in his own places. See you later, oldsters.

I checked on him as much as I could. He was in a rock band, and they were rehearsing in some other kid's parents' garage, lucky for us. Gary said this was our reward for merit in a past life. They played a loopy form of neo-punk cacophony, with Eli's Brit

CDs as hip models to copy, and Eli was the manic, poker-faced drummer. He went and got a blue Celtic chain tattooed around his arm, but he promised to stop there. I told him piercing and hair dyeing were okay, but not tattoos. I threatened to wear a nose ring if he got another one, just to embarrass him. He did think that was funny. He could be so charming on his good days.

The Yosemite hike had been arduous in spots—I wasn't in quite as good shape as I'd thought—but it left me with a craving for more. After the first trip, I took off by myself on these long hikes whenever I could—back to Yosemite and to Lassen and to Marble Mountains—but not when Eli was home, only when he was away, in England with his mother or once with a friend's family on vacation in Oregon. I never felt right about leaving Mattina to deal with Eli by herself. She wasn't ever completely his parent, and I didn't want Eli pushing the envelope on this while I was gone.

The hikes always had miserable patches—I got lost more than once and wandered around scared and my leg muscles couldn't believe the steep terrain that presented itself—but I was usually happy when I sat down to my lunch on some boulder with a nice view. How strangely slanted those days were, the chilly mornings with their hazy light, the speechless days, the long nights in the tent with its smell of dirt and damp canvas.

I began to want to go on longer hikes alone. Three weeks, a month. Gary filled in for me at work without too much griping.

"Why live with other people at all," Mattina said, "if withdrawing is such heaven?"

"I come *back*," I said. "I don't want to retreat all the time. Believe me."

"Which is more real to you?" she said. "Not us, I bet."

"Mattina," I said. "Don't worry, I'm here."

"Say something nicer," she said. "I feel like a needy nag, for Christ's sake."

Not for the first time, I thought it had been selfish of me to marry her. "You look gorgeous," I said. "Every time I come back. You do." She did.

When Eli arrived home from England at the end of the next summer, he was smoking two packs of cigarettes a day. "Only Americans are these lame health freaks, " he said. Mattina gave him a hideously graphic description of what happens to cancerous lungs, and we tried to ban him from smoking in the house. "In the U.K. people smoke anyplace they want," he said.

"Next you'll say you were crazy for Bovril and baked beans on toast," I said. But Eli's attachment to British habits meant the summer with Peggy had gone well. She was living with a journalist who wrote for some scandal sheet, a much better guy than the last lager lout she'd been with, and they'd taken Eli to the cold English seashore, which he had actually liked. "You just take walks, you don't have to lie on the beach all the time," he said. He could never resist brightening under whatever light Peggy shone on him.

Peggy looked older, in the snapshots Eli brought back from those windswept walks on a craggy coast. We were all getting older, there was no news in this, but Peggy's face had grown leathery and coarse and disturbingly gaunt. The change in her

felt like an outrageous loss to me, although I never saw her anymore. She was always planning to come back to the States for a
visit, but she was always short on money or full of complicated
neurotic reasons—she had to have her teeth checked, she had to
be in London for the solstice, she wasn't going to fly with a lot of
college kids when it was spring break.

Eli said that the two of them had talked about his going over
at Christmas for another visit. That was fine with me, if Peggy
meant it—I hated her getting him all eager and then changing
her mind, as she had done before. But I wanted him to go—to
have more of her, if he could. They were great fans of each other,
at this moment, and I wanted him to get the best of that. Eli
smoked and drank and slept with girls, but he was just a kid.

Through the fall, Peggy phoned pretty often. The trip seemed
to be on. From London Peggy and her boyfriend were going to
drive Eli in their tiny clunky car to visit some friends in Bristol
and then maybe head into Wales—Eli would really like these
places, Peggy said. I bought Eli a leather bomber jacket for the
colder weather, and he bought a sequined scarf to give his mother
and a cowboy shirt for her boyfriend. I had to help him guess the
size on the shirt.

I was busy before the holidays, at work too much of the time.
Then we had trouble getting in touch with Peggy. At night I was
too overworked to sleep, and while Mattina lay next to me, I
heard Eli talking into the telephone at ungodly hours of the
morning, the best time to reach his mother across the ocean. He
had his ticket, he just wanted to tell her when to pick him up at

Heathrow. He had been leaving messages for several days and she wasn't calling him back. "Just checkin' in again," he kept telling her phone machine. He was working at sounding casual and not forlorn.

I didn't get anywhere either when I called her at breakfast time, but I barked a scathing speech into her message tape. "Listen to me, Peggy. You always think you're the only fucking person in the universe. What has to happen to get you past this dumbass delusion? When are you going to get it? You're not the only pebble on the beach."

Afterwards I knew I sounded sanctimonious, and I thought Peggy was only going to be inflamed by this hectoring. I was afraid that she might decide not to call back at all, just for spite. Was she spiteful? Or was it narcissistic of *me* to think my effect on her could be as mighty as that? I got so gnarled up in the twists of this question that I broke a carved marble statue I was moving from one part of the store to the other. It was an angel that once had been on a grave, and it lost half an alabaster wing while I was deep in thought and not paying attention.

Probably, I thought, Peggy was just going to call at the last minute, surprised that we had ever doubted her. But Eli was nervous, and his room became a cocoon of noise, a vibrating monument to the booming technology of amplifiers. There were only three more days left before his scheduled departure, so we let him do it. I didn't know what else to give him.

Mattina and I hung out in the yard, which was only slightly quieter than the house, and we argued about whether Eli could be coaxed into leaving the premises for Mexican food, which he liked. I heard a repeated trill that was either the phone or something in the music, and Mattina made me go in and check.

I had to ask the person to wait while I yelled at Eli to turn down the volume. "Tom?" the voice said. "Tom?"

It was Rita, Peggy's mother, sounding weird and expressionless. The trip is off, I thought, Peggy's delegated her mother to be the apologizer, to bring her bullshit excuses to Eli. I had a flash of pure hatred for Peggy.

"I have bad news," Rita said.

"What?" I said. "What?" I had to run to tell Eli to make the music softer.

"Okay," I said, when I was back.

"I have bad news," Rita began again. "About Peggy."

She told me Peggy had been driving to the country for the weekend, with her boyfriend in his little car, and when they were leaving London, not even outside the city yet, a truck came out of an underpass. "A huge truck," Rita said. "It pushed them off the road. Just like that."

I heard myself moan.

"They took her to the hospital," Rita said, "but it was too late. No, that's not right. She was in the hospital for an hour before she died. I think it was an hour. I can't remember everything."

Had Rita gotten any of this right? She often got things wrong. For a second a wild scorn for her puffed me up with false hope.

The man had lived for two days longer, she said. But it had

taken the American Embassy five days to locate Rita in Illinois. "Me, her only relative," Rita said.

But I was thinking of Peggy, strapped into a small, tinny car in a ditch. We had to talk about which of us should tell Eli—I said I would—and whether he would want to go to the memorial service in Chicago.

As it happened, Eli had heard most of the conversation—there was never any privacy in that house—but I had to look at him while I said it again. He was trying to hold his face together, but his mouth kept slipping into weeping. Then Mattina came in and I had to tell her. It was somehow decided that we would all go to Chicago together, and suddenly we had a lot of work to do about getting airline tickets right before Christmas and finding hotel rooms and canceling Eli's other flight and packing and calling Eli's school. I was caught up then in a wave of duty, a wave of listed tasks, and underneath that surge was the pressing, unrolling urgency of Peggy's death. I had to do all these things—now, fast, without failing—as if they could save her.

I HAD NEVER even been to Chicago. Peggy's hometown and I'd never visited it once—I kept thinking about this on the plane. Had I ever known Peggy? But I thought that I had. She was with me now so distinctly; she had been in my mind every second since Rita told me. Wearing a blue lace bra she'd had in London, or asleep on my shoulder on the bus in Thailand, or in our old apartment in New York, nursing Eli on the couch. Part of me was

pleased (although that is not the right word) to know she had
died in England, in a place we had a history together. I had a
claim on that part of the world, where I had flung myself with
such recklessness into the certainty between us.

> *So, after all, we have not*
> *failed to make use of these spaces, these*
> *spaces of* ours. *(How frighteningly great they must be,*
> *since thousands of years have not made them overflow with our*
> *feelings.)*

On the plane to Chicago none of us talked much, and that
was fine. Eli stared out the window and didn't even put on his
Walkman. Mattina read the airline magazine for hours and let Eli
drink the beer she'd ordered. We landed in the kind of frigid winter temperatures I had forgotten about, in all my years in
California. Only Eli, in the leather jacket he'd bought for
England, wasn't shivering in the wind when we walked down the
jetway. I held Mattina under my coat to keep her warm.

It was twilight when we arrived, and the memorial service was
the next morning. None of us wanted to do anything but crash out
in the hotel. I'd gotten Eli his own room and he disappeared into
it. Mattina and I lay in bed, watching CNN on the TV. Experts
were arguing meanly about tax proposals. "When you were with
Peggy," Mattina said, "was that a time you lived more deeply?"

She caught me by surprise, although she asked quite gently. I
shouldn't have been surprised. "Things between us were always
dissolving," I said.

This was true enough, and I could see Mattina took this answer well. But it was a trick answer too, a Buddhist answer.

I kissed Mattina all over her face, to soothe her and to show her she had me for her own, which she did. After she fell asleep, I stared into the dark and I shed my tears for Peggy and for what we hadn't had. She was never going to be my lover again. I should never have gone to California, should never have left New York, all those years ago. I was sure now that that had been a mistake. I was bitter against myself for that.

And yet I would have said—I always said—that leaving Peggy, getting free of her, had brought me into a truer, fuller life, caused me to make better use of myself. I knew this. I would have traded any of it at that moment to bring Peggy back. It was my luck that no one ever gets a choice like that.

In the early hours of the morning, I thought I heard Eli's music coming from the room next door in a fog of jittery noise. Why wasn't he using his headphones? Well, he wasn't. Mattina stirred in bed and said, "Our Eli." Peggy had been a flighty, capricious, and cruelly uneven mother to him, but she had loved him intensely in her way. He was listening to a tape of his band or one like it. I was sure that Peggy wouldn't have minded at all being mourned in those pounding lines of percussive force.

I myself had been trying to meditate, to wish Peggy well, wherever she was. I'd been awake for some time doing this. At first I thought I heard Eli getting dressed (so early?), but then I was fairly sure that he was dancing. Nodding to the music, with his eyes closed, twitching and sliding. I knew how he looked. And he was smoking a cigarette while he danced—the Indian herbal kind he liked these days, with a scent like flower incense that wafted into the hall. Peggy, being dead, could not see us, but she would have been glad at the sight: me sitting cross-legged on the floor, Eli dancing in his underwear, the two of us in our frost-windowed rooms in that somnolent hotel, making peace with her absence as well as we could. I was thinking of the lines Rilke wrote for his own tombstone,

Rose, oh pure contradiction, joy
of being No-one's sleep under so many lids.

IDEAS OF HEAVEN

I was still quite a small child when my father went away to fight for the North in 1862. I was so little they had to explain to me over and over why he had left us, why President Lincoln needed him. I was impatient for my father's letters and very excited when they arrived. I would jump up and down and run through the rooms of the house in a way that I was not allowed otherwise. When we didn't get a letter for a month, my older brother Fred scared me by being scared himself. He said that since our father was the regiment's doctor, who would tend him if he were hurt? Who would stanch his bleeding or dress his burns? One night when my sister Maude, who was almost grown, lay in bed next to me, I dreamed I saw my father in heaven. Perhaps it was not really a dream but an idea I was turning over in my mind. My father seemed very present, very near, and had apparently been this near to us for some weeks, like a pet we had not known was in the house all along. The sight of his face made me realize how long it had been since I had seen his own true features, but now he was purely there, himself.

In fact my father was not dead. The mail was held up for weeks, but he was home safe by summer. My brother Fred called me a little cheat for having had such a dream, but I believed that I had had a true glimpse, however blurred and shaded, of another layer, hidden and precious, always lurking nearby. I was too little to think about this clearly, and I could not hold on to the sense of it very well, but the dream was mine, and I kept it.

FRED WAS MY favorite, of my siblings. He used to write me letters, once he was away at college, full of sentences in languages he liked to pretend he had mastered. "*O oktapodi darlino*—as we say in Greek—hello, my darling little octopus." "*Nolite esse amens goosus.* I hope you're paying attention, Lizzie, that's Latin for don't be a silly goose all the time." I was fifteen by then, but he still thought of me as much younger than I was. It surprised him when he brought home a friend at Christmas and the friend seemed to enjoy talking to me.

We lived in a small town, not far from Hartford, and it was Easter when Fred came home with his friend Bennett. Maude, who was married by this time and living on a small farm, played the piano in our church. When she took up "The God of mercy be adored,/ Who calls our souls from death," the roll of it swept over me with a freshly triumphant meaning. I was quite lifted up at the time anyway, because I had been talking to Fred's friend all week.

He asked my opinion on a number of subjects, although I could not talk about much except the amusing things the younger children had done while under my care. I asked about his studies, and he said that philology was making him more religious. I could make no more sense of this sentence than if he had baa'ed like a sheep. "Do you think there is one God over all people?" he said. "Of course," I said. Bennett said that an Englishman serving in Calcutta in the 1780s had found very many words in Sanskrit that were so like Greek and Latin that their similarity was surely not a coincidence, and scholars thought this probably proved we had once all spoken the same language. "I am sure we all did," I said. "How could it be otherwise?" I had long felt that the earth was linked by a great net of glorious strands.

And so we began to write back and forth, Bennett and I. Sometimes he enclosed little puzzles and jokes for my sister Phebe and my youngest brother Lawrence. I sent him sketches I had made of my father's horse, Scipio, and of the vegetables in the kitchen garden. Everyone liked Ben and thought he had a pleasant way about him. After a few months of these letters, my mother asked me when I thought Ben was going to declare himself, but no one really thought he was a trifler. My sister Maude made fun of my sketches—"what man wants to look at a portrait of a parsnip?"—but everyone was glad enough when Ben proposed, and we were married just past my seventeenth birthday.

———

I HAD THOUGHT a great deal about what love was. I believed that the deep affections of my own family and what I had felt on occasion as the radiance of God were connected, that the human version "participated" in the Divine. I was away from Bennett during much of our courtship, and I walked through the streets of our town during those days with a great longing to be in his arms, to rest against him. I was not ignorant about physical love, but I had not quite understood the way that this diffuse yearning would locate itself so pointedly in the vital tissues of my body, once Ben was actually with me. And perhaps I was startled most by the changes in his body (that being the aspect I knew the least about), by the swollen, hardened flesh rising from my Ben, the gentlest of men. He was as much a novice to the act as I was, and we rowed through these new waters together.

I saw why a man and wife must never leave one another, having been to these places in each other's company. Afterwards I thought about how I might be a mother, at any time now, and it seemed right to me that there was a state so much like fever—a spell or a melting fit, a possession by great forces—that was the portal to this realm.

MY MOTHER SAID that Ben was good-tempered but impractical, and I would have to be a careful housekeeper, which she knew I could be. After we were married, we went away to live at Briar Field Academy, where Ben taught the younger boys. He was very patient with his pupils, though I was afraid that the bigger students were often spoiled and willful. "Don't be outraged for me, please, Liz," he said. "It makes me wearier."

I missed my parents, but Ben's were nearby and we had Sundays with them. After church, his father and brothers would talk about the sermon, as if it were an urgent piece of current news requiring their remarks. My own jolly family had mocked my earnestness, and so I quite liked the tone of these talks.

And on several of these afternoons I was secretly sure that I was expecting a child, and so the seriousness of the world was something I felt very keenly.

Each month when I saw I was not pregnant after all, I knew myself to be a silly woman who had fooled herself. I did not pray to conceive, because I had been taught by my father that petitions were a superstitious use of prayer. He always scorned people who thought they could pluck at the Divine sleeve for particular favors. I kept myself busy at home and I gave myself what counsel I could.

Later, of course, this seemed like a carefree time to me. In the seventh year of marriage I had my first baby, my sweet James, and only a year and eight months later I had my beautiful Lucy. There was no question of hiring a servant on Ben's salary, and I had no idle moments anymore—indeed I could not remember what I had once done with all my leisure. But I had become a fairly cunning manager of our household economy, and I did quite well for my poppets, I thought. They could toddle and run about on the school grounds in the open air, though James was sometimes too rough for his sister. Ben made them a toy wagon—a wooden crate with pot-covers for wheels—and they liked to haul horse-chestnuts back and forth in it.

One winter afternoon when James was almost six, Ben came back from walking with him by the river. Bits of snow were melting on their coats. Ben said to me, "I don't know how people live without a sense of God." I said I thought such people's lives must be vapid and tedious, without color or depth.

He and James had come across a bird on the path—a starling with its legs up, stiff and frozen. James, who was fond of birds, had asked if it was dead, and Ben said he thought so. As James drew nearer the feathered corpse, he said to his father, "But *I'm* not going to *really* die, am I?" We had just been telling him that Jesus' resurrection proved that goodness was more powerful than death; his mind was tender and responsive.

"It made me remember," Ben said, "how many people all over the world look at a dead bird and feel only dread for themselves and a natural horror of decay. I think they must live always with a taste of horror."

I knew the movements of my husband's thoughts and what he meant by *all over the world*. A young cousin of Ben's had just come back from serving five years in a mission on the south coast of China and he had talked during Sunday's dinner about the unrelieved misery of the people. When Ben first said "without a sense of God," I pictured only the vain puffery of some of our coldly prosperous neighbors, but Ben's notions roamed across a wider field. It gave me a queer feeling to think suddenly of China instead.

———

I HAD ALWAYS known that none of us would have been Christian if the Disciples had not gone out and made nuisances of themselves among the Gentiles. The next evening, Ben wondered aloud what it might be like to serve in an overseas mission as his cousin had, and we began to have conversations, night after night, in which we tried to reason from this rash hypothesis. Fright crept over me often, yet I felt very steady. How plain and sober my Ben was, tallying the risks (the unhealthful climate, the years away from people we loved) and the beauties (to see someone feeling for the first time *what* Christ was, to know one had done this one good thing in the world). In the end all the reasons against going had a selfish grounding, we both came to think. I liked those suppers, the long deliberations, and each of us looking to see what the other truly meant.

IT TOOK two years until Ben resolved on doing this, and the night after he said to me, "Shall we go then, my girl? I think you must know we are going," a kind of mental breathlessness came over me, a delight that floated on fear. My old life was opening into something quite other, which I could scarcely yet recognize as my own. And when my father wrote to me, "Oh, Lizzie, why are you setting off on this stony path? What have you to do with the Orient or the Orient with you? I had not thought two homebodies such as you would be so reckless," his worries seemed to me part of a pettier, narrower, greedier world that I had already left behind.

I was expecting our third child by the time we moved to Oliver, Ohio, where Ben entered the Congregationalist seminary at Oliver College and prepared for ordination. I had my most difficult birth in those rooms in Oliver, a wrenching labor that went on for two and a half days, but my husky, funny Douglas was a healthy boy from the first. At the christening Lucy asked me if babies in China cried in Chinese, and I told her all wailing was the same, like dogs howling at the moon in every part of the earth. Even at the baptism we had the thought of going abroad always with us, like a root fire underground, a radiant foreboding.

WE WENT THROUGH all our savings, such as they were, in those five years in Ohio, and at the end Ben applied to the Board of Foreign Missions to be sent to China. We were older than many of the other mission volunteers, less fresh and blooming, and we were afraid that the Board might insist on a softer posting for us, but they did not.

We were assigned to Shanxi, an inland province in the north, and asked to think of staying ten years. My parents came to say goodbye, before we took the train to California. My mother wanted to repack everything for me, while Douglas, who was only three, pulled out all the cups and saucers from the trunk and Lucy kept trying on my shirtwaists; the general family pandemonium distracted me most conveniently from the sorrow of leaving. My father gave me some seeds for pole beans and nasturtiums, and he waved his hat as the train pulled out of the station. He looked so glum to see me go.

We were five days on the train to San Francisco, and then six weeks on the ship, where I was sick as a pup most of the way. But when we got to Yokohama, Japan, our first sight of Asia, I understood that facts are more solid than we can stand. Every particle of strangeness was perfectly real—the jinrickshas with men trotting in front of them like horses, the dead volcano with its snow-capped peak looming over the city, and the crooked streets with their rows of open-fronted shops. All of this had been here all along, the tree falling in the forest while I did not hear it.

We were eight days in Yokohama and then we took a steamer to Kobe, and from there two weeks on a bigger ship. I woke all of us very early, so that we would be on deck to see the shores of China before we docked. The sky stayed white after the sun came up—I was told that the sky in China was always white—and the land coming into view was misted over so that it looked poetic and oddly inert. The children were quiet, for once, except for Douglas, who had to be fed sesame candy to keep him from restless agitation. A Mr. Thomas Comber, one of the returning missionaries, told the children to think of the horizon as the *sky's edge*, which was how it was written in Chinese. Ben had to go ashore with Mr. Comber to buy provisions for the rest of the trip, and I could see that he wanted me to go with him, and I suppose I was eager.

The men working on the docks turned to look at us, as well they might, and I guessed how unnaturally shaped we must appear, me in my long, stiff skirt and the men in their hats and buttoned jackets. Most of the Chinese workers were shirtless, wearing only loose trousers, their braided queues falling on their bare backs, a brevity of dress that would have startled me at home. In the harbor, and farther along the alleys of dark wooden houses, there was a terrible reek of human sewage and animal rot. The odors were no less as we moved closer to the main part of town, and although I was thrilled to see more people moving about, their faces full of their own unknown Chinese business, it was very hard to have the smell as my first great impression, although we managed better in the shops than I would have thought. Ben and I pointed at sacks of meal and beans and held up our fingers, with Mr. Comber helping a little, and the merchants grunted and weighed and wrapped, as if nothing surprised or much interested them.

We had more traveling to do, on the river for five days in narrow houseboats. There was no wind to fill the sails, and the boatmen had to pole us forward in the muddy, sluggish water. Their bodies seemed frail and skeletal to me, and yet their efforts moved us along the banks, hour after hour. Any man who was relieved of his shift fell asleep at once, sitting on deck with his head thrown back.

James kept hoping to see water snakes and insisting to Lucy that every motion in the water was one. I dreaded the next two weeks with the children, overland on pack-mules across rocky terrain. But as it happened, the freshness of the mountains did all of us good, and Douglas, who had fussed quite a lot on the boat, sat nicely with me in a litter that was like a big basket strung between two mules, whom we named Mister Lovely and Mister Snort.

I HAD TO wait until we reached Fenzhou, the end of our journey, to be alone with Ben. It was a small city, old and dirty and poor-looking. The mules stopped before a street entirely fronted by a high brick wall, and it was not until a guard unlocked a massive gate for us that I understood this was the missionaries' compound.

A couple who introduced themselves as the Rexroths and who looked very young came out to greet us and Mr. Comber, their old friend, and we were very glad to see them. But I was sorry to find there were no other children here. The outer door was locked behind us at once, and I supposed we were safe, though I did not like being shut in.

There were inner gates as well, with horrid stone dogs guarding them. No one had told me that our "house" was to be, not a house at all, but a group of cell-like buildings lined up around a gray brick courtyard. Only the moon-white windows, dark-paned in cunning geometries, saved these from utter bleakness. Our rooms were dusty and long neglected, and I had a good deal of work setting out linens and bedding, our own dear things from home. One of the kitchen boys tried to help me, and I almost wept from trying to make him understand what I wanted; he would not beat the dust out of the pillows for me and he would not go away either. I put Douglas to sleep first; he was tired, as we all were, but he would not lie still until I told him the mules were tucked in too and Mr. Snort was snoring like a trumpet.

I should have known that when I was alone with Ben, he would want to keep talking, as he did when he was stirred with excitement. "*Women xiang yao liang bei cha,*" he said, one of the first phrases he had learned in Chinese. "We would like two cups of tea." Already it seemed to me that the language itself, spoken so rapidly around us with all the words run together, was a vast sea, a froth of tides we could only drown in. No wonder the work here went so slowly. It was truly a sign of special power that any Chinese at all had taken in the teachings of Jesus and not assumed they were nonsensical rantings. "*Women xiang yao,*" Ben said again, moving the pitches up and down in the second word and barking the last in an exaggerated way. "*Liang bei cha,* Liz."

"You sound very fine," I said, as if I had any way to know.

"They say it takes a year," Ben said. "To learn enough to go out and preach to people. But I can go with the others to hand out pamphlets."

It hurt my heart to think we had come this far just so that Ben might ply people with papers he could not even read himself, hawking his broadsheets like any pesky newsboy at home.

"I cannot like living inside a fifteen-foot wall. What are we locked in against?" I said.

"I suppose there are bandits," Ben said. "And beggars and wild dogs. Everyone has a wall here. Any house in the town bigger than a shack has a high gate around it. Edward Rexroth said two bandits were caught last month and beheaded in the town."

How had he become the expert so quickly, and I the student?

"When you go out to the villages," I said, "how will you keep yourselves safe on the roads?"

"No one thinks it's dangerous. And the others have been going out in Chinese dress, to show we don't set ourselves off from anyone here."

I did not see that any outfits would make them safer. "Who will make a Chinese gown for you?" I said. "Am I to do it?"

"Only you," he said. "A long gown with two cups of tea stitched on it, please. *Liang bei cha,* my girl."

Being happy sometimes made him silly and effusive like this. He kept me up a long time with his talking, though I could not be cross with him on this our first night. It was very late when he stopped, and after he led our prayers, we had our time together as man and wife, which we had not had on the road. And then I was glad to sleep, with the feather bed from Ben's mother's house laid out beneath us. I was going to be in this room for the next ten years. My bones were very heavy to me and I hated to think of ever getting up out of this bed.

Just as I was falling out of consciousness, a live thing whirred and streaked through the dark air of the room. It slapped against the windows. "It could be a bird," Ben said, "but I think it's probably a bat."

I knew it was a bat, and I was not afraid of bats either, although I had never met a Chinese bat. We listened to it beating itself against the wall and then it swooped and dove too close to the bed. "Get *away*," I said, as if it obeyed any language.

"It only wants to leave," Ben said. He got up to open the door for it and I heard him mutter when he bumped against one of the spindly little tables. Something crashed and shattered on the brick floor—I knew it must be the hand-mirror with roses painted on its porcelain back, a gift from Maude when I was fifteen, but still I hoped it was something else. The bat seemed to hate the sudden noise and in its flailing agitation it brushed against my cheek— this was like being smacked with a leather glove, and I cried out. Ben got the lantern lit at last, and the two of us ran about trying to trap the frantic body of the bat in a quilt. We pitched it out into the courtyard. Lucy began calling from her room—"Why are you shrieking? Who has come for you?"—and I let her stay with us awhile to calm her, while I swept up the glass and tried not to think how long our time here was.

THE REXROTHS gave us breakfast the next morning; their Chinese cook made a perfectly decent millet porridge. When we told the bat story, the incident turned quite comic, with Ben the blundering hunter.

"A broken mirror is seven years' bad luck," Jamie said, being a boy who relished dark matters.

"Not in China," Thomas Comber said. "Surely not. And a bat is a happy sign here, don't you know?"

"Please don't make fun of us," Lucy said.

"It's true," Susan Rexroth said. "Because the word for good

fortune is said exactly the same way as the word for bat, though it's written differently. So you often see bats depicted in the most splendid embroideries of gardens. The Chinese are very fond of that sort of pun."

We all felt better for this information, though we had heard time and again how badly encrusted with superstition the Chinese nation was, how its progress was hampered by old beliefs. I think if there had been a way to set out a dish of milk for bats, we would have done so at once.

ON SUNDAY MORNING I had the experience of hearing Thomas Comber preach in Chinese. The other congregants were three workmen from the town plus the kitchen boys from the mission households and the Rexroths' cook and her lively four-year-old daughter. And our own family—the service took place in the dark sitting room I had hung with curtains of blue-and-white toile. Thomas wore a skullcap and what I called a "Chinese gown," like a cassock, with a long brocade vest over it, and he did not look laughable in this outfit so much as patient and put-upon. I was suddenly and stupidly amazed, like some rustic booby, to hear him rasping and piping syllables in Chinese and know they signified the news about Jesus. When he used a name or phrase I recognized—Galilee, baptism—it was very moving to me. I could not tell if any of the Chinese were much affected or could even follow him. I thought how badly God wanted them. How mangled and crimped their lives were. And how if they understood Him, they might spring free, just like that, from the pride and greed that knotted them now in humiliation.

Douglas was fidgeting during the service, and the cook's daughter began to prattle out loud. So before the final hymns I had Lucy take them both out to the courtyard, where the cook and I came down afterwards to see them chasing each other like romping dogs. The cook hobbled on her bound feet, but when she laughed at the children, she had a pretty smile, with one chipped white tooth. Later I said to Ben that I thought her walk was an emblem of this place, the tread of a woman unjustly crippled and laboring onward, in ignorant forbearance. "Well put," Ben said.

"You might wait to form impressions," Edward Rexroth said. "Placid is not any way I would describe the national character."

THE FIRST MONTHS were lived almost entirely within the compound. I did not like to think I was afraid to go out, but I was. When Lucy and James were done with their lessons and Douglas was napping, I often went up a set of stone stairs that led to the roof, and I took in the view of the ancient, miserable town, with the gray mountains hovering over it. According to Susan, the cook thought we had all come here because it was so much more pleasant than our home. The streets were lined with high brick walls of a grim gray color. From the roof I could see now and then a bit of traffic in the road: an old woman with an enormous basket of squash strapped to her like a rucksack, a child bent under a stack of firewood, a man trudging behind a wheelbarrow of bricks. A city of hunched backs and no prospects of better.

Ben spent many hours of the day studying Chinese, and a boys' teacher from the town came in to tutor him. Thomas Comber warned against going too fast; there was a famous case of a missionary in the early days who lost his reason from too many concentrated hours of study, though I myself thought it must have been a wider frustration that tormented his mind. Our own mission had been here for three years, with only two reliable converts in a city of thousands. I studied too, but I learned the most from our kitchen boys and from the cook's daughter, Chunhua, who played with Douglas every day. The two of them got along very well, though I worried at how dirty she was.

China was hardest on Lucy, I thought. James played tennis at the net Ben set up in the courtyard and he went out to villages with his father, but Lucy had a dull existence. It was autumn when we came, and through the winter, I would talk to her about the garden we were going to set up in pots in one of the courtyards. She helped me make a list of the seeds we wanted sent from the U.S.—zinnia, morning glory, bachelor button—and we kept my father's nasturtium seeds away from Chinese mice. "Is heaven full of flowers then?" Lucy said. "Or is that only an idea people have?" I thought this was said from longing, since we were in such a bare and leafless spot.

"Heaven is the answer to longing," I said. "All our hungers are met with the love that we're too hardened to do more than taste fleetingly now." I thought this was not too difficult for an eleven-year-old.

"Then flowers are my own sign of heaven," Lucy said. "James can have goats for his heaven."

We had just gotten a pet nanny goat, whom James was very taken with. After this I had Ben buy a finch at the bird market for Lucy, yellow and brown with a black beak, and he bought a rabbit for Douglas.

WHEN THE WEATHER grew milder, I took Lucy for outings. We went with Susan Rexroth to visit some women in a house in a neighboring street. They were a merchant's wife and her sister and elderly mother, and they had come unannounced to see us the week before, in long cloaks and flowing trousers, their faces dusted with white powder. They had been very eager to see our sewing machine—I sewed a pocket on an apron to amaze them—and they opened all our cupboards and looked into the drawers of my desk. Their faces crumpled and smoothed in different expressions, but I could not tell what they thought.

When we went to visit them in their house, with its elegant square-cut furniture, they gave us tea, and asked us our ages, a question we had enough language to answer (I had not known Susan was *ershi,* only twenty). They showed us how their hair was done, pulled and twisted and fastened with hairpins as long as chopsticks, and wondered that we did not fix ours that way. Lucy asked, mostly in pantomime, if they would put hers up like that, and for a little while we were like schoolgirls anywhere, fussing and tittering. Who would guess that our vanity would bring us close? I wondered if they loved their men, to primp for them so, though I could not ask them that. (Best not to ask anyone, for that matter.) All their marriages were arranged, and yet people told us the country's literature was full of love poems. I thought their feelings must drift in two streams, the unfed ideal and the cruel usual. Though they seemed the most practical and hardheaded people. Just before we left, the old woman brought in a tray of magnolia blossoms, and we bent our heads while she pinned them to our hair, so much wispier and weaker in color than theirs.

Lucy looked like a beautiful toy, with her freshly lacquered hair and her flower. On the walk home, a group of young boys passed, and I thought one was staring at Lucy in impudent admiration, until I heard him say, "*Yang guizi*. Foreign devils." The other boys took it up, jeering and making rude faces, though they did not chase us. I would not let us walk faster, because I did not want us to look cowardly, but I was grateful to reach our walls. Ben said later that they treated us better than Chinamen were often treated at home. This was true but not what I wanted him to say just then.

THE SUMMER was very hot; the mist over the rooftops might as well have been steam. The smells in the streets made me afraid of exposing the children to infection, so we stayed inside, though the air in the courtyard had no coolness to it. Our garden flourished in the hot sun. We had planted grass seed in the one unpaved courtyard of the compound, and this was now a little field where Susan and I played croquet with the children. Susan was a finicky and intense player, who could take several minutes lining up her mallet. She looked much older than her age, she had lost a three-day-old infant in the year before we came, and the games brightened her.

Ben played too, and the children were vastly amused when he hit a wild ball and it skittered off and broke a pottery jug. Susan said the sound made her think of an Englishwoman she'd met in her early days here, who had walked through the countryside smashing idols. Douglas said, "Oh! I wish I'd seen her."

"What theatrics," Ben said. "The temples are deserted as it is. There's no need."

"She meant well, I suppose," I said.

"I did like to go with her," Susan said, "though she always thought I was not zealous enough."

Ben and I often talked at night about what form *zeal* should take in this place. We had seen from the first that a very long patience would be needed here. After all the semesters at the seminary, all the savings used up, all the talk night after night about a hundred million souls in China. We had to cultivate a different ardor, a suspended thirst, like a lover who waits years for his beloved to come to him.

My brother had asked in a letter if we had any sport here besides singing hymns. At the moment, Susan was so intent on croquet that she wanted us all to postpone lunch. She was not persuaded until Douglas rolled on the ground in what he claimed was a fainting fit from being famished. It was too hot to play after we got up from eating, but Susan and James were fierce competitors, and they took up their game again, wiping perspiration from their faces as the afternoon wore on. James was a good sport when Susan won, and he made a victory crown for her out of an old American newspaper, folded like a hat. Lucy said it looked like something his goat might wear.

OUR NEXT YEAR in China was a much better year. Dr. Langston, a homeopath, and his wife Leora came to live on the other side of the city, and they had two boys, one of them close to Douglas's age, as well as a dog and a canary. More people from the town began coming to services, and though some were not sincere (a few items disappeared from the house), six or seven did seem to want truly to be baptized. Everyone in our mission traveled to Taigu for the Annual Meeting, and we felt ourselves great adventurers, marching into this bigger city in our mule carts. I was very glad to see other Americans and I talked on and on about small matters, for the sheer pleasure of it. And new visitors came to see us at home—first a single lady from Scotland who was passing through on her way to Tianjin and then two Swedish men who had been living in very rough country near Mongolia. We used up all the cans of butter the Board sent to us from San Francisco and had to eat biscuits without it for months till more arrived, but the suppers with guests were fine times for us.

Ben found us a cooler place to live in the summer months, an old mill near a stream, with trees all around it and an expanse of terraced fields in view. Local people came to the window to watch us while we ate, but from their staring I thought they at least learned how we lived. We had beautiful walks in the open air and picnics on a hill. When Lucy walked with me, she said a woman on the road wanted us to know the fields were planted with white poppy (the children understood more Chinese than I did). In Taigu Lucy had seen men and women addicted to opium, when we visited a hospital where they lay in a ward, wasted and hardly able to move, waiting to be cured if they could be. The fields, ready for harvest, were quite lovely, with their seedpods capped with pale green pads.

I had been sorry in Taigu that I'd brought Lucy to see those hollow, ravaged faces, and Ben and I had argued later about what should be expected of a mission child. Ben was willing to drive all of us hard. I did want my Lucy to be of use in the world. What is the point of being human if we do not give ourselves to the full task of it? But I sometimes thought of sending her to live with my parents. She had turned twelve before the summer, and while she still had the looks of a girl, I did not like to think of her becoming a young lady here.

One afternoon Ben took the children on a long walk to the far end of our stream, and James caught a beautiful, glistening carp. Thomas Comber was visiting with us, and at dinner, when I served it with white sauce, he said fish meant abundance, another of those Chinese puns from words sounding the same. "It's my fish and I'd rather just eat it," James said. "All this business of everything having a hidden code gives me the flim-flams."

"It could mean an *abundance* of anything. Of fleas," Douglas said. Fleas were a problem in our beds.

"A drawing of a fish was a signal for the early Christians," Ben said. "You know that, James. That was how they let each other know where they were meeting. Because the letters for the Greek word for fish were the initials for Jesus Christ, Son of God, Savior."

I heard James whisper to Douglas that he hoped the boiled potatoes did not have a secret meaning, and Douglas went into a brotherly fit of sputtering giggles.

I had a mouthful of carp while some of this conversation was going on, and I wanted my fish to be only simple food too. I wanted just to chew. No one lives that simply, I thought. Not here, not anywhere. Everyone is always straining to see a web of connection.

And didn't I myself believe that earth and heaven were constructed according to a holy design? Yes, but I did not believe that I could see it. Not in this life.

And I was glad that James did not have an analytic temperament. I wanted him, and the others too, to be contented in the meal Lucy and I had made—her peach pie was next—and in the pleasant summer evening, whose soft green scents came through the window.

"There are no potatoes in the Bible," Ben said, "but I happen to know these are the exact biscuits they ate in Eden."

"When people use opium," Lucy said, "how is it they cannot eat?"

"They cease to concern themselves with food," Thomas Comber said. James said that was a poor version of paradise, in his opinion. When I looked behind him, I saw the faces of three men, peering in through the window, staring at us in what seemed to be endless curiosity, and I thought we must make quite a nice picture, just as we were.

WHEN WE CAME back to Fenzhou, Ben began to talk about having a school for boys, like one we had seen in Taigu. He wanted to throw himself into some work of his own, apart from the other men, who did not always get along. He talked to the few friendly Chinese in town who were not too poor to pay a minimal fee, and by January we had seven boys from these families boarding with us. Ben taught the boys their catechism, and we hired a Chinese teacher for their other lessons. We let Douglas play with the younger boys, and James helped his father teach, but I kept Lucy away from all of them, as much as I could; the older boys were in their teens.

Chunhua, the daughter of the Rexroths' cook, was Lucy's own pupil. I would hear Lucy trying to explain in Chinese what the Sabbath was, a thing unknown in China. It was hard to know what Chunhua made of all this, but Lucy was very attached to the girl, and carried her around like a sack of meal, with the girl squealing in glee. She called Lucy *jiejie,* big sister. Lucy taught her to sing "The God of mercy be adored," which she rendered in a shrill voice, blurring the syllables. I tried my best not to laugh. Her mother said the music alone was enough to scare away any bandits in the vicinity. She was a dear woman.

Susan Rexroth was expecting her first child, and I taught the cook to fix beef tea and soft puddings to nourish her without upset. I would coax Susan into taking exercise by walking up and down our street in the early evening; we talked to the Chinese women who sat in doorways with their babies, and the four of us strolled along, Susan and Lucy and Chunhua and I. In the thinning light, I felt (though I didn't say so) how much more at my ease I was than when I had first come, and Susan, naturally enough, was in a cheerful state of mind.

WHEN WE CAME back one evening, the cook, Azhu, was in the courtyard, sitting in her padded jacket, waiting under the lanterns for her daughter. She asked if we might tell her just one thing about the crosses we wore. We were very happy for any such question. We couldn't quite follow her Chinese, but she seemed to be wondering why we wore sets of gallows as jewelry (we did know the word for execution). We tried to tell her our own rough version of the Passion, which sounded gory and fantastical, as it must have been. There we were, two sober matrons and a tender girl, speaking of blood and torture and unstoppable love. Azhu looked quite startled, and then she carried Chunhua off to bed.

A week later Ben told me Azhu had asked to be included in the lists for eventual baptism. All our talk of suffering had struck her. Perhaps she had been turning in this direction for many weeks, and our answers had had little to do with it. But it was one of my best moments in China, when Ben told me.

O N   A   C O L D and nasty November morning, Lucy complained of headache, and in the middle of the day she lay on a sofa with a cloth over her eyes. I needed her to help with the ginger cake (she always made the desserts), and I was about to tell her not to be dramatic when it struck me she might be near the start of her first menses. She answered petulantly when I questioned her about symptoms. But when I put my hand on her cheek, her skin was distinctly hot, and so I let her nap.

By evening she was shivering with fever and clasping her forehead in pain. Ben carried her upstairs to her own room, and we put quilts over her, but her teeth chattered as if she were in the Arctic. James went to get Dr. Langston, who said that we should keep giving her water to drink but otherwise let her sleep. In the night she looked astonished each time she woke, her eyes glazed with disbelief that this attack was being visited on her.

In the morning a red rash appeared, as if a scalding iron had been applied to her face and chest. The rash seemed to spread before our eyes. And then we knew. "Did a louse bite her at any time?" Dr. Langston said. "Typhus comes through lice."

"Don't be afraid," I said to Lucy. It was my fault that she had played so often with Chunhua. Why had I never stopped her, why not?

"Steady on, girl," Ben said. "God has not left."

We did not let the other children in the room, but James sent in her finch in its cage. It made a twittering racket, but the children knew to expect certain indulgences when they were being nursed. Lucy grew more childish under her fever, laughing hoarsely at the bird and pulling at my hand if I tried to leave her bedside, calling us by pet-names she had not used in years. All my children did such things when they were sick, but I was frightened that Lucy was falling through time, slipping down away from us. Ben said this was a morbid fancy. The mild depths of his voice when he was praying in the room were sometimes quite wonderful to me.

By the fifth day, I could see that Ben was becoming more alarmed, though he was still the best at soothing Lucy. I bustled too much, and she turned her head away when I offered cool water. "You *have* to drink," I said. I was angry with her. When she closed her eyes, her whole face seemed to shut, and I had a spell of being frightened of my own child. She was becoming something I knew nothing about. I understood that I was an innocent now compared to her. She twitched and shifted under the covers. "Are you all right?" I said, an idiot's question. Still, I felt better for asking it.

Lucy did not answer me—why should she answer? All my grasping and fluttering and flapping were not, at this moment, to the point. She was not very interested in us at present; she seemed busy elsewhere. When I watched her closed face, I had the sense to be in awe. She was so clearly working at something.

When Ben came into the room (looking old, with his streaked mustache), he asked me if she was sleeping, and I said that she was *occupied.* "Is she?" he said. We watched her as we might have watched a figure on the road in the distance. The next days were not so hard for us as I would have thought.

ON THE EIGHTH day we went into the parlor to tell James and Douglas that their sister had died. Their faces were terrible to see, and very little we said could lighten their anguish, though I thought if we could get them not to be *afraid,* we would be doing our best for them. I let Douglas sleep in our bed, though he was seven and old for this. But then I worried that James was in their bedroom all alone.

The Chinese carpenters took as much care as they could hammering together a coffin, and I had the kitchen boys dig up a corner of the croquet field to make it ready. This was the only ground that was ours; there was no church nearer than Taigu, too far to go. James and Ben went out to the flower market and brought back pots of roses and two young trees, a willow and a red pine, for the boys to plant before the service.

Thirty Chinese came to the service, more than had ever been inside our compound at one time. It did me good to see them file in, row after row in their long tunics and webbed sleeves, quiet (for once) in their soft-soled shoes, except for the tap of the women's canes.

Ben and I worried that James, who had been Lucy's nearest

companion almost his whole life, might be unsteady during the service, but he was upright and composed. It was Douglas who sniffled and wept; Susan had to keep whispering to him. Afterwards, when we were giving refreshments to the assembled group in the yard, we got both boys seated on a bench and I gave them tea and lotus-seedcakes someone had brought.

"So many people are here," James said.

"We have a form of hope that they don't have," Ben said. "It is something, that they can see that."

Douglas started to cry again when he saw Chunhua, who had her hair done up in ribbons.

"You will make the others sadder. Try to hold fast, if you can," I said. "Douglas?"

"We are all going to die eventually," James said. He was trying to be manly, but I wished he had not spoken.

"Death is not the same to me as it was before," Ben said to them. "It is not so terrible, I think."

The children looked upset when he said this—I thought they did not like to hear a father so consoled—the words were only what he and I had been saying to each other, over and over. The agreement was sweet to us. But they were too young for that sweetness.

AFTER THE FUNERAL, I did not like to see Douglas playing with our Chinese students, but I couldn't have stopped him or the Langston boys either. I knew that I was wrong to blame

China, as if there were no such woes over the rest of the earth. I'd had a sister, two years younger than Fred, who died of diphtheria before I was born. I didn't want to speak too much of any of this, because Susan Rexroth was having her baby in a month, and we were all happy for her too.

Douglas, who missed Lucy very badly, was excited when he heard Susan had gone into labor. Hours later, she gave birth to a tiny, round-headed boy, and Douglas was allowed to hold him when he was a week old. I was pleased that Edward Rexroth allowed it; he was a stiff man whom I did not understand well, but he was softened by delight and he could not refuse anyone. Chunhua sang her loud hymn to the baby, who was too young to have musical opinions.

After a month, Susan was induced to leave her baby with Azhu, her cook, just for a short spell, while the two of us went for our pleasant walk through the streets again. The baby was not ready for the outside, since Fenzhou was in deep winter, but I thought Susan and I both needed to move about, to stir ourselves. When we rounded the corner to come back, we could hear her boy crying, and the sounds were quite loud as we were let back in through the outer gate. In the kitchen we found Azhu with the infant in her lap; she had unfastened her tunic and pushed aside the binding cloths beneath it, and was trying to comfort him by giving him her dry breast. "Please!" I shouted. Susan and I both went to snatch the baby, but I was faster. "Please, *never*," I said.

The cook's face was pinched tight with hurt, and Susan had to say we knew she meant only kindness. Chunhua was crying too, from hearing her mother scolded. The baby would not settle down for a long time, no matter what anyone did. Susan walked him up and down, while he wailed. Chunhua looked at me in horror.

THE NEXT SPRING, seven new families asked to be baptized, and Ben said it gave him solace to think that Lucy's funeral had helped to bring them to God. He said this often to me, and I heard him say it again when were eating dinner at Thomas Comber's. I had thought a good deal about Christ's sacrifice and the fearsome beauty of His example. It was a notion I had lived with for a long time, but I did not think it made sense to very many Chinese.

"You are wrong about that," Thomas Comber said. "The Chinese are very attracted to sacrifice."

We had all read in the English newspapers that Japan's victory over China in their brief little war had fired up people's anger against all foreigners, and in a province near us, one group had torn down miles of telegraph lines in its rage. "In this miserable country," Thomas said, "people are desperate to give themselves over to a higher principle—as well they might be, don't you think?—and this idea has got itself mixed up with wrecking and pillaging."

"Oh, they're just foolishly nostalgic here, in ways we don't even see," Edward Rexroth said. "The ones who rip up the railroad track—what has the railroad done to them? But they believe in a lost paradise, before the foreigners came—they think they can get it back."

"It is hard to think of paradise in China," I said.

But I thought of a Chinese paradise as soon as I said this—the intricate and perfect gardens depicted in their embroideries, and the actual, careful gardens that grew behind the walls of people's houses. When Lucy and I paid our visit to the women of the merchant's family, we had glimpsed—through a moon gate—dark-branched magnolia trees with cups of white petals, group-ings of bamboo and rock, stalks of blue iris near a pool of water. I was tempted to picture Lucy now in such a place. But I did not think anymore that heaven was a place. I liked to think of Lucy as beyond the ill fit of *places,* outside the walls of the visible. Free.

After we came back from our summer home, I packed up Lucy's clothes and sent them to the mission Board in San Francisco, where some other girl might find them useful. I sent a few keepsakes back to my family—Lucy's Chinese shawl and the long carved wooden hairpin the Chinese women had given her—since I wanted them saved but did not like to see them now. In the first months after Lucy died I had walked about in an odd state of clarity, where nothing in her going from us was unnatu-ral or cruel, and I'd been grateful for this clarity. I was all right then. I was less all right a year later.

Ben was often out again in the villages, talking to people and passing out tracts. I would have liked him more at home; our families in the States had begun sending us worried letters.

Farther south, along the coast, ten English missionaries had been horribly murdered, by an obscure vegetarian sect with no ties to where we were; my mother, who read of this in August, did not fully understand how big China was.

Nor did James, as it turned out. We were doing lessons together one morning and he seemed to think that Connecticut was the size of Mongolia. A great boy of fifteen, almost sixteen. He tried to make a joke of it, saying that Connecticut had put on flesh since last we'd been there, but this irritated me too. He had spent these years playing with the Chinese students, who would not cross him in anything, and with Douglas and the Langston boys, who were all much younger.

I spoke to Ben about it when he and Edward Rexroth and Farley Langston came back from the villages, sweated and dusty from being jostled in a donkey cart. "He'll be an egotistical ignoramus if we don't take him in hand," I said.

Ben said I was always finding trouble where there was none; he wanted only to bathe and rest. "I wish you would listen to me," I said. "Just a little."

I watched James more closely in the next few days. He spent hours tending his goat, who did not need much care, and asking the Chinese boys their Bible questions—there was considerable disorder in the class, but some of the older ones recited the right answers. When they did not, he was at a loss and could only read out the correct lines loudly.

"What will he do in the world outside?" I said to Ben.

I had the idea that we might take him back to America, to

study at Briar Field for his last year; I thought Ben's family would be very happy for us to stay with them awhile. And then we could get James settled with someone to learn a trade. We might ask the Board's permission to leave China early; other people had done that. Once I got hold of this thought, it was with me every minute, though days went by before I voiced it to Ben.

Ben said he would be ashamed to leave so soon, and he was disappointed to hear me speak of it.

"I could take the boys back without you," I said. "Both of them. And you could join us in another year or two."

Ben's face drained of all its vibrancy when I said this. I had cut him badly, as I must have known I would. "Why are we a family then?" he said. "Why have we bothered to link ourselves?"

THIS QUESTION KEPT burning in me, as if it were the title of a sermon I was writing. I wanted so badly to go, but I had to answer this first, it seemed to me. I tried to think of any people in our mission who were solitary. There was Thomas Comber, who had learned the best Chinese of any of us and who ate his meager meals alone and spent his evenings at his books. But he must have felt the lack, because he was now engaged to marry Anna Esther, the single lady from Perth who had passed through here two years before. And there was Li You, the boys' teacher, who had no family in the district and few ties in the town because he was a Christian. He was a quiet figure, though he was known to beat his pupils. I admired his sticking to Christ even unto friendlessness.

And could I have done the same? I would not have come to China alone, as some women did. Love of Ben had brought me here, bound up with my older feeling for Jesus, a simpler love. I had never thought to be anywhere without Ben. But now the thought of leaving here had become to me what opium must be to people who sell whatever they own for it.

It was no good arguing, Ben was not changing. I was sick quite a lot the year after we quarreled about this. I had some digestive trouble and then a long bout of bronchial illness. Douglas had bronchitis with me, and I was afraid for him. But once his fever was gone we lay in the big bed all day and played games of checkers on a board we set up on the quilt. Li You brought us rice porridge with red dates to strengthen our systems, and Susan's cook Azhu sent over peaches stewed in honey. James and Ben took over the housework, with the kitchen boys at their usual labors, and I thought I might stay in bed for the rest of our time in China and no one would mind either.

But I had to get up once Douglas was better. When I went out again, the streets of Fenzhou seemed worse than dismal. Susan had been helping Farley Langston in his clinic and she came back with terrible stories. A family with an infant who died on the way home from the clinic threw the dead baby girl outside the town wall for the wolves. A poor farmer had a son with a gangrenous leg that needed amputation, and he was so angry at his son's uselessness that he ordered a coffin made and was ready to bury the son alive. The smell of the streets was hellish when I thought of these things. The weather was bad for crops this year and a rumor had spread that the missionaries kept rain away by fanning very hard at the clouds. We did this in the nude, apparently, as part of our other unspeakable orgies. Also we took the eyeballs out of orphans' sockets to use in our cameras.

James had taken over the care of Lucy's pet finch and while he was taking it outside in its cage for an airing, as people did here, some boys rained pebbles down through the bars and injured the bird. James ran home with the poor thing making piteous squeaking noises. He tended it as well as he could; it was like looking at a sentimental drawing, to see him put salve on the little finch's wing and stroke its feathers. Chunhua gave it sesame seeds to eat. I was surprised when the bird recovered. Perhaps I should not have been surprised that James was clever in something.

BEN WHEEDLED the money out of the Board, for my sake, and we had workmen come in and transform the house into something much more habitable—new flooring, new walls, the gray brick pavement dug up for more gardens in the courtyards. Our Lucy would have liked the gardens. I wrote the details to my family—I drew them floor plans, I sketched the arrangements of the furniture. James teased me about my "big story."

I thought of the Dickens I had read as a child, when the theatre manager in *Nicholas Nickleby* brags of a performance by his wife so remarkable it had to be discontinued because "it was too tremendous." A boy of James's age might be expected to see a comic element in such letters as mine. And yet I thought of my life as a "big story," with much dared and much expended, with airy heights and echoing depths, and set with illustrations as garishly colored as any child's Bible tales.

BEN AND JAMES were together a good deal in the year I was so often sick. They began to call each other Chinese nicknames—*lao wazi* and *xiao maozi,* old sock and young hat. I was glad to see Ben diverted. The sight of him jostling and joking with James in the donkey cart was very charming to me.

So it surprised me when he wanted to send James home. He spoke of it as if it were my idea. The Langstons had announced they were moving on to another posting on the coast. And, in bed that very night, Ben said to me that they might easily take James with them to a port in Zhili where he could board the boat for home. "He is not a baby," Ben said. "He is old enough to be on a boat by himself."

"He's past the age for Briar Field."

"Somewhere near my parents there must be a veterinary surgeon he could attach himself to. Or something else. Since he's not to be a minister."

"You could stand to be without him?"

Ben did not answer. It was good of him to let James go, I saw that. And when the two of us talked to James the next day, all the sulkiness left his face at the thought of going home.

I had not thought this too would be asked of me. To have James taken from me for the next five years, if we all lived to see

each other. Douglas was upset too, and had to be kept from kicking at the bushes in my garden. He was losing the Langston boys
as well; I had to remind him that his life was lucky compared to
many. But a group of tiny chicks he was raising had just been
eaten by a rat too, and I was sorry that we were not giving him a
more innocent childhood. I thought China was a nation with
hardly any liking in it for innocence. How soft and witless we
must seem to them. Small wonder so few were drawn to Jesus,
with all our talk of His sweet unstained mildness.

IF THE WEEKS of preparation were agitating to Douglas,
and sorrowful for us, they burdened James with an excitement
that made him sometimes loud and overbearing. Li You said he
was like a drunken puppy. In the end James acted embarrassed to
leave us—"You will keep on working so hard," he said—and I
felt an odd surge of pride that I was staying.

DOUGLAS WAS SAD at being left behind, and I did my best
to divert him. A week after Halloween, which we celebrated with
a few carved round squashes, Anna Esther came down from
Taiyuan and as soon as she was out of the cart, she said, much too
quietly, "I have something terrible to tell you." A flash of pure
pain shot through me, and I took Douglas's hand, but the news
was not about James, as it happened. In Shandong, a province to
the east of us, two German Catholic priests had been murdered

by a small armed band. What band? How murdered? "A Chinese gang was robbing them," Anna Esther said, "and you will not want to hear the details." Some people thought it wasn't bandits but one of the secret sects that always made trouble for rulers.

There were many reasons not to worry, and we all said them aloud to each other. Shanxi was known to be a peaceable province. Catholics interfered in local courts to help out their converts, which other Chinese resented, and we never did that. We had not run a railroad through anyone's sacred graveyard or brought bad luck to the city by building on a wrong-facing site. And none of us (Ben pointed out) were interested in pouring poison in wells or removing the organs of babies, despite the rumors. We repeated these reasons in every conversation with one another for weeks.

IN THE EARLY SPRING the city of Fenzhou was suddenly crowded with men who had come to town to take the civil exams. We could hear waves of them outside, walking in the street. Susan and I did not leave the compound, but Ben went out as always.

At lunch Ben came up the stairs to the room where we were eating, and he was holding a bloody handkerchief over his eye. "I'm all right," he said. "A man threw a clod of dirt at me. Several men." Just outside the city wall, he told us, a group of more than a hundred men had surrounded him, hooting and pushing. When the dirt-throwing began, he'd resolved not to run. A boy from our street had come up to stand by him, a brave boy, and had led him home by the narrow back-streets, so the crowd could not all follow at once.

My own Ben. I put a sticking plaster on the bruise and tried not to be flustered—I could see how frightened the Chinese students at the next table were. They lived in a tiny Christian world, like a scene in an eggshell, and their teacher could not keep himself from being mobbed and pelted. Ben said a round of prayers with them and I gave them extra fruit and some nut brittle the cook had made. They let us quiet them.

"WHY DO THEY hate us here?" Douglas said to me that night.

I reminded him of how the Pharisees and the Romans had hated Jesus, because people can't stand to be rebuked. "We're not in the Bible," Douglas said.

"We are always in the Bible," I said. I suppose we lived, in our way, outside of history, and now we were made to face the mystery of the temporal. It was never very clear to me what the foreign companies in port cities or the opium sold by the British or the disgrace of lost wars had to do with the poor farmers out here in the countryside, or with us. "It is all enraged pride," I said to Douglas. "A sense of insult makes them vicious."

"They oughtn't to throw dirt," Douglas said.

———

WE WENT ON as always, with our services in Chinese and our great Christmas dinners for the boy students, but fear was always with me and had become my great teacher. It made me more tender to my husband, and it let me entertain (that was the right phrase) my longings to see Lucy. There was no more trouble, but there were reports of trouble in other places.

Anna Esther told us that in Shandong many people thought that the telegraph wires, which they knew carried words, were strung with the tongues of murdered children. "They are very literal here," she said. They heard moans when the wires moved in the wind and saw blood when rusty water trickled down the poles. "It is the poetry of dread," Ben said. "We give them the willies," Douglas said.

I had lovely letters from James, who was speaking Chinese to the horses at home and skating on the river with girls, insisting on instruction from the prettiest (he was a breezy writer). I had only the weather to write him about—cold wind in winter, with much dust blowing about, and very little rain in the warm weather. The second summer of no rain was especially bad, with the yellow-brown earth so cracked and bare that the millet and wheat couldn't be planted. We had more beggars at our gate, and it was costing us much more to feed the boys at school. James said he treated a cow with a prolapsed womb and bathed in a creek attended by adoring tadpoles, though the letter did not arrive until Christmas.

Susan's son could count backwards and forwards in both languages, without faltering, and when the year turned 1900, we let him count down the seconds for us, in his little scratchy voice, though we celebrated at noon, when it was midnight at home. In the midst of broad daylight I was as mellow as any reveler, standing next to Ben, quite flooded with feeling to think of how many New Years we had had together. My heart was really very full all through the prayers.

IT WAS NOT more than a week later when Ben came to me in the kitchen after the post arrived. "I think you had better sit down," he said.

He asked me if we knew a Sidney Brooks, an Englishman, and it was some moments before I stopped thinking the man had to do with James. This Brooks had been on horseback traveling to his mission in Shandong, and had been stopped by a gang of men who belonged to the Boxers, a group who'd been harassing foreigners and converts. They had beaten him and stripped him naked in the cold, and then they'd made a hole in his nose and strung a rope through it and led him around for hours. His dead body had been found in a ditch, riddled with sword wounds.

I felt there was something wrong with me, that I had no way at all to understand how such a thing could happen. Had this been on the same planet that was my own habitation? A patriotic frenzy had turned these men to demons. I took hold of Ben's hands and for a while we sat without talking, like a shy courting couple.

"The twentieth century is not beginning so well," Ben said.

———

WE AGREED NOT to tell any of the children the details, but they could not help hearing the broad outlines. Douglas kept asking if the Boxers wore gloves, but Thomas Comber said that was just our own name for them. They practiced a martial art, like the exercises people in Fenzhou often did in the square, but the Boxers went into trances and fits, visitations they thought made them invulnerable.

What a lurid world God has given us, I thought, how teeming and loud and crowded with unfurling shocks. I wondered if Jesus had been astounded continually, or if He moved over our tawdry earth without any amazement.

Li You said he was sure the government would put a stop to all the trouble with the Boxers. I wrote pleading letters to newspapers, in Ohio and Connecticut, telling about the drought and asking that emergency funds be sent at once to China, describing the leanness of people in the streets and a man who'd been living on leaves. "They send money?" Li You asked, but he knew the letters would not even get there till late spring. I cut back on our dinners, with their courses of soups and pies, and we stretched our hoard to feed two Chinese families who were temporarily staying with us.

When I went out to visit a woman with a sick infant a few streets away, I saw new posters on the town walls, but I could not read them. Ben, who was with me, translated the characters. "Uphold the Dynasty. Exterminate the Foreigners," he read, quite softly. "Only Then Will Rain Come." A man pushing a wheelbarrow full of long cabbages walked right by the poster, the same as always. But on the way back, I saw a drawing of a man in a shirt and trousers roasting over a fire, pierced by the lances of scowling soldiers. And I would not go out at all, or let Douglas out, once I'd seen that.

By the end of May our Chinese couriers were not carrying letters out or in; they came back saying roads were blocked by the *I Ho Chuan*—the Righteous Fists of Harmony, as they called the Boxers—and word was out that a man caught with a packet of foreign writing had already been killed. The telegraph poles that linked us to the world had also been knocked down, the couriers said. We were cut off from help, if we needed it, but I thought we had better stay where we were anyway. There were still no incidents in our town, except for the chilling posters, and we could not desert our own Chinese. We did have arguments about this in the compound—Ben and Edward Rexroth were bent on staying and Thomas Comber would have left if he could have. Susan's boy Timothy, who was not yet six, was curious to see the Boxers. I said I hoped he would not have a chance.

In June Ben went out to bring medicine to a man with an infected eye, and he came back with a look on his face I had never seen before. "They are here," he said. From across the road he had seen two Boxers in the square, in their white tunics and red sashes and red headbands, and they were leading a drill. They were very young men, and they'd drawn in local boys as young as ten. They called out incantations and bowed to the south, towards a shrine on Peach Flower Mountain, and then all of them—the whole group—fell backwards onto the dirt, rolling their eyes. When they rose up, they went into fits of pantomimed fighting, like the staged battles in their operas. A woman from our street told Ben they were shouting the names of gods and figures from legends, whose strength was in them now.

I was glad I had not seen it. In our dull little square, people were frothing at the mouth and stabbing the air. We might have found them laughable, if they had not been dangerous. Ben said he thought that in time the Boxers would move on, this was not a place for them. Perhaps he believed that.

The town magistrate issued an edict against them—edicts were very powerful here—but a day later signs were up revoking it. He was a new magistrate, with a long face and intelligent eyes, and he more or less liked us, as far as we could tell, but he had to placate the governor of the province, who thought foreigners were ruining China. I wrote to my brother Fred that the politics here were as treacherous as Caesar's Rome. I wrote to James that the students were all leaving us, one by one, and that his goat had eaten my summer hat, the straw boater with the finch's feather in it. I saved my letters, to be sent later if we lived or if we didn't.

What had I been doing all these years if I had not learned how to die? I wanted so much to be in a frame of mind where the question of dying did not weigh on me, and my sense of His glory was the strongest of my feelings. When we were praying with the kitchen boys and the cooks, in Chinese and in English, I had a few minutes of freedom and lightness. I could not think why I had ever worried, and I hoped they saw it, our own Chinese.

———

LI YOU CAME into the compound one morning very agitated, muttering and shaking his head—he had just seen an imperial edict posted on a wall, announcing that in three days all foreigners were to be killed. Ben and Thomas and Edward went out at once to the magistrate to plead with him. They came back tight-faced and confused. "He was very calm and very friendly," Ben said. "He told us the edict was all talk."

No one knew what to think. Susan, who was pregnant again, kept saying she hoped that our own armies would come to save us. "Where are they then?" her husband said. Ben had a shotgun for hunting and a revolver for killing wolves; he took them out and cleaned them. "Have we come to China to murder people?" Susan said. "All this way to kill Chinese?" I suppose I did not like to think of being with Ben after he had done such a thing. All of us discussed this for an entire day, and in the end I brought out the garden spade and we wrapped the guns in oilcloth and buried them by a red rosebush. Douglas patted down the soil and sprinkled dry pine needles over it.

I spent the next day packing a trunk, in case we had a chance to get away, and we put whatever money we had in a strongbox, and Ben hid them both under straw in the chicken house. On the day of the ordered executions, we read the Bible and sat with each other and waited. There were noises from the street but they were not new noises. I wrote letters to James and to my parents and to my brother Fred. I talked to Lucy in my mind. Ben dug up the guns and cleaned them again. I stewed rhubarb and strawberries from the garden, and I had the boys sweep out all the closets. I had Douglas do his sums. Ben practiced his calligraphy. We waited through the night, and when dawn broke, we saw the day had passed, and no one had come for us.

AND SOON THE telegraph line was working again. There was a wire from Baoding, and no one knew why it had been directed here. "Do you know, it's in Latin?" Ben said. "I suppose no Boxer knows Latin."

The men translated together, interrupting each other. Thomas Comber's Latin was the best. "*Solum spes yoreciv statim imperat mittere milites. Sex mille pugiles ad orientum liu obsidentes Romanos,*" they read. "Our only hope is if the viceroy orders the General to send soldiers. Six thousand Boxers are at Tung Lu village besieging Romans."

What Romans? "Roman Catholics," Ben said.

He tried to send a message out to Tianjin for help, but the lines were down again. He kept trying, but the lines never came back.

THOMAS COMBER wanted to ride to Taiyuan to get Anna Esther out. None of us thought Thomas could survive on the road long enough to save anyone, if she even needed saving. She might well be safer than we were. Thomas was induced not to try, but he was always at the stables, and I saw him praying while he stood by his horse.

Every foreigner in Beijing had been killed; every foreigner in Beijing had been rescued by a vast fleet of the British navy; the Empress Ci Xi, who was sixty-five, had a lover who was a Boxer. There were too many rumors; we had no one whose word we could rely on, and we were shut in with our own ideas. We made a rule that we would not talk about the Boxers after the midday meal, though we did speak of the *pugiles*. I did everything I could to be calm in front of Douglas, who had all his toys and books stacked by his bed next to his packet of James's letters, ready for flight.

Li You played catch with Douglas in the courtyard for hours. It touched me to see the Chinese who stayed with us, who chose not to go. We had done something in these years, I had to think, to bind them to us. Azhu still cooked for Susan the delicate soups she liked to eat when she was pregnant.

Our carpenter had word from a cousin that in one village, Chinese Christians had been buried alive by Boxers. When the servants heard these stories, they sharpened all the kitchen knives; they wrapped their queues inside headcloths so they couldn't be seized by the hair. Our kitchen boy looked like a tiny pasha, and Li You's eyes were fierce under his turban.

There were tales of Boxers asking people to urinate on a cross drawn in the dirt, and cutting off the heads of those who would not. I heard this without flinching, but at night with Ben I began to weep. "What have we done?" I asked, as if my poor husband had to answer. For years we had talked of how the Word was so often watered with martyrs' blood, but we had said this to gird ourselves, not to wish it on anyone else. What a dark chapter of the Bible we were in.

The town was now full of posters ordering all converts to recant. Everyone knew that in a village close by, four converts had been beaten with clubs by the magistrate's men, and made to bow in front of idols in a temple. Thomas Comber asked if it was a Buddhist or a Taoist or a Confucian temple, but no one knew. "The magistrate had them beaten," Ben said, "to save them from the Boxers."

"You think he is clever, do you?" Edward Rexroth said.

In the morning I was working at the stove with our turbaned kitchen boy, frying squares of cooled porridge for breakfast, when I heard something rolling over the dirt of my garden. It was Chunhua and her mother Azhu, both pushing a wheelbarrow with their belongings in it. They spoke to each other, but not to us, though they saw me. We were already dead to them, love was dead. I had such a mix of anger and sadness at seeing them leave, I could not think what to say. I would have liked to give them something, but I hoped they were not stealing anything we needed.

A week later we heard that a district official had been killed while he was trying to arrest a group of Catholics in a village. I did not mourn him, but Ben said the governor of Shanxi, whose name was on the Boxers' banner, could appoint whom he liked now. Our local magistrate would be helpless under his rule.

All that day, the Chinese who worked for us moved about the compound, rolling their bedding, loading sacks, strapping baskets on their backs. The sun was very hot and I would have pitied them hauling everything they owned in such heat, had bitterness not been creeping over me. Now we had nothing to show for our years of work; soul by soul, they moved through the two sets of gates and out into the street.

By nightfall Li You and two other men were all that remained to us. In the morning a note came, saying that we were going to be sent out of the city and escorted to the coast.

"Escorted to safety?" Susan said. "Can that be? It could be, couldn't it?"

"Oh, my dear," Thomas Comber said.

They were providing an escort, we had only to hire litters and mules for ourselves. We did not have anywhere near enough money for this, and the next day when Li You went out to raise cash, someone had pasted on the city walls a new decree from our own magistrate, "Kill Foreigners."

Li You told this first to Ben, who came to me while I was picking pole beans from the courtyard for supper. "It's very plain, isn't?" Ben said to me. "No hidden meaning for us to parse here."

He looked baffled, his face twisted into a deep squint, contorted from thinking what God meant. He took the shovel from my gardening tools and went into the chicken coop and came out later with the money box. There was no point, he said, in any of the Chinese staying with us, and we had to give them something to leave with.

———

WE ALL STOOD by the inner gate to say goodbye to the three men—Li You looked quite undone when Douglas shook his hand. Thomas Comber came out of the stables with his mare, and he walked her over to the man who had been his housekeeper and gave him the bridle.

That night I dreamed of Lucy. Ben and I often had dreams of her, as people do of their dead. In this dream Lucy was giving us tickets to America, on a steamship that could skim over land and had come right to our door in Fenzhou. The boat was full of bats, who flew out of it into our faces, opening their black mouths, spitting and shrieking, and I would not board, and Lucy told me not to worry. When I woke up the fright was still in me.

By noon the next day Li You had come back to us—his knocking at the gate alarmed us at first. He had a plan to help us escape, by a wagon into the mountains. Guards had been posted outside the compound walls, but he believed we could slip out at night. Ben said that we should try if we could, and he got the others to agree. I said that I was ready to die but not through rashness.

Was my husband a rash man? My family had thought he was too modest and weak, though they changed that when the idea of China got hold of him. In China he had often thought better of people than I did, but he was never imprudent. I had to ask myself now if he was a fool for hope, a goose who flapped his wings at the merest crumb.

He had already grown old in hope's service; his hair was entirely white, his neck webbed. Old sock indeed. He was still wearing his long Chinese vest and calling his tea *cha,* even now when no escape could ever make us disappear into the populace. But we were tied to the Chinese, I did think so, as we were tied to all humans, though the net was barbed, the net was choking us.

S O I D I D N ' T argue against Ben in any of his plans. All of our men were struggling to do whatever they could. They had Li You give silver to a man who promised to go to Tianjin for help, but the man disappeared. They had our belongings smuggled out so we could pick them up when we got out, but the cart was stolen. It all ended when the magistrate got word of the escape plot and and sent his men to confiscate our guns. Then we really had nothing.

We were left to wait. Susan was in her ninth month and I was in the kitchen alone, working to feed us, drowning in my own sweat. I was hanging the laundered sheets out in the back courtyard when I looked across to Thomas Comber's doorway, where he was speaking to a Chinese woman I had never seen before. She was dirty and her pants were torn; he went into his house to bring her a melon he had from our garden, and then she walked out the back gate. When I called out to find out what was going on, he put up his palm as if to stop me, and turned and went back inside.

I was afraid to guess what this was about, until Susan came to me later. In Taiyuan, which the woman had just walked all the way from, the Boxers had set fires all around the mission compound, and the sparks spread from the gate's roof to the buildings inside. Anna Esther had been fleeing, helping a student with newly unbound feet, when she slipped and fell and people pushed her into the bonfire. The Chinese woman had seen her get up from the flames and walk away to pray, but the crowd had thrown her back on the burning pile, and then a door and a table and boards were stacked on top of her, so she could not get out.

Susan told me this in a kind of whisper, as if it could only be uttered as a secret. I thought of how the world had always held such things, Jesus knew them. They were like a hiss under all speech. Ben came in when Susan and I were clasping each other, and she said we were envying Anna Esther.

THE MAGISTRATE SENT a notice to our door—we were now expelled from the city. Edward went himself to plead for a delay until Susan had her baby. He came back wincing in anger, saying, "What people are these?" Li You was sent to ask for an audience for Ben. I said how brave You was to go, since a man had just been lashed eighty times across the face for not addressing the magistrate politely enough. Li You was told if we did not leave the next day, the city would send troops to flog us out.

We had no money to hire carts to carry us, and where could we walk to? How could we carry food and lead the children? The government was going to seize our houses, so we couldn't sell them. I sat with Timothy and Douglas and told them we were going to wander the desert like the Jews in the Bible but in time we would come to a sparkling oasis that overflowed with everything we could want. I knew this for certain. Douglas gave me a knowing look, and Timothy was confused but satisfied.

It was Thomas Comber who managed at last to arrange to sell our summer house in the mountains, the old mill by a stream with its shading of willows. He got us a tiny allowance for it, and so we hired carts to take us out.

I WAS SO busy getting all of us ready, I did not have time until midnight to go out to the garden with Ben to take leave of Lucy's grave. I was not so superstitious as to think she was truly there—no, she was elsewhere—but I was sorry to leave her behind nonetheless. Troops were going to be housed here, Ben told me.

What are we leaving behind? I had been asking all afternoon while I was assembling what we needed to take. Ben kept saying he was sorry we had not been able to do more here, but I had my sentiments attached to each room. I did think our ghosts were in this place, the ghosts of our broken ardor, but the spaces were so ancient these could scarcely tint the air.

In the morning, the carters came in through our gates and loaded our baggage. Then we climbed aboard the carts, sitting on the slatted seats like chickens in a coop. When the second set of gates opened, the sunshine flooded in on us, and we could not help feeling glad to be in the open again.

Soldiers on horseback rode ahead of us. On either side of our street were throngs of people, as many as could fit between the walls and the road. The crowds continued for blocks; I had never seen so many Chinese in one place. Ben said he thought there were thousands—all of Fenzhou had come out to watch us leave. People stood on rooftops and on the ledges of walls. They were silent in their attention; I thought they all wanted to remember the time they saw the foreigners driven out.

Once we had passed through the city gates, a fresh breeze rose up over the fields around us. The sorghum, which had survived the drought, grew in grassy stalks five feet high. The cassia trees were in bud, and for once the sky was a cloudless blue. Douglas stood up to look out, as if we were on a summer excursion. Susan said, "That was a very large group that came out to wish us bon voyage."

I said, "Our soldier escorts have handsome uniforms too." I had not thought we would be bantering.

LI YOU WAS in the back of the cart, with Susan's Timothy clambering over him. Ben had told You he should not stay if he could get away, but he could not seem to bring himself to leave us. Timothy was interested in the soldiers' horses and wanted to know if they were sweating, which made Li You laugh. Douglas sat with the breeze ruffling his hair; he was very still for an eleven-year-old boy. I was full of regret that we had not sent him home with James.

The day grew hotter as we bounced along the road, and Ben asked me if I wanted my umbrella. When I said no, he handed it to a soldier, to give it to his leader to keep the sun off him.

At every village we passed, people came out to stare at us. When we stopped in one spot to water the mules, I saw a man selling melons, and I sent Ben out to buy some for us. The fruit was fragrant and cool in the heat, and we all sat eating it as if we had no concern more urgent than picnicking.

When the carts started up again, we were on very rocky road, and I worried at Susan's being pitched about; we could do nothing but mound piles of clothes to cushion her. Timothy crawled over us to find his mother and fall asleep against her side. Douglas was singing something under his breath, a rhyme about a poll parrot.

Lucy's finch was back in Fenzhou, released from its cage to feed in town on grains in dung. I should never have had children, I thought. Though my best love had been for them, we should not have brought them into our audacious project. It should have been Ben and I alone, living without family. That would have been fairer.

I looked back to see the road vanishing into the horizon and I did not see Li You's back. No one was sitting where he'd sat. He wasn't in the front with the carter either, or in the other cart with Thomas and Edward and the baggage. He had slipped away, taken a chance when he'd seen it. This was not a good sign.

We went through another small, parched village, with everyone in it standing to watch. Outside the town we came to a sorghum field, and the carts stopped. Ben put his hand on Douglas's shoulder. There was the loud thud of a single gunshot somewhere ahead of us. Let it happen quickly then, I thought. And as if I had ordered it—but I was already screaming to wish it back—men were rushing towards us, coming out of the brush and the cover of trees with swords in their hands, shouting. We were yelling to God to save us, though we knew we would have to be shattered to get to Him. The men were running to us, their faces wild as wolves', their arms reaching to thrust and cut. Our deaths were pulsing in us, like Susan's baby in her body, our sweet kingdoms within. The first man to reach us struck Thomas on the forehead with his sword and left a bleeding gash. We have to help him, I thought, over the clamor, but men were streaming forward—I put my arms in front of Douglas's face, and a blade slashed at them. The pain made me cry out, and then my head was smacked, over and over, and my neck was weeping. I couldn't see where Ben was. Why was there so much blood? Why was it so hard to get across this gate? I wanted the other part to begin. I had such longing. We were so near. We had to be shattered to get to Him. I closed my eyes for it to begin.

THE SAME GROUND

I wasn't really surprised when my older brother Yves wanted to be a priest. He had always been the most earnest of us, and our family had some history of sending its sons into the priesthood. My mother had a cousin at a church in Lyon, and two generations back there was a great-great-uncle with the Benedictines who survived the siege of Peking in 1900. So Yves probably thought of doing such a thing from the time he was quite young. Although none of the other boys in the family had any such ideas—we were not priest material. But he was, we all felt it.

When he came back home to Dijon after his first semester in the seminary, I peered at him for signs of change—I wanted to see how much of him I had lost. He was still wearing his Yves-clothes and his Yves-cut hair, everything trim and nondescript. But I was eighteen and I thought he looked already somewhat sexless, somewhat lacking in dash and vitality. He had been a good soccer player, an agile boy with strong, square shoulders. I was sure that he was softer now, though he claimed not. How could he contemplate an entire life without a chance of ever sleeping with a woman? I had had a year of sporadic joys and could not go for an hour without thinking of them, much less imagine forgoing them forever. In those years I could not have asked my brother if he liked men, but I thought he did not.

He seemed happy and even excited about his life at God-school, as the rest of us called it. He still joked with us, and we insulted each other as we always had, but our enthusiasms must have seemed pale and inessential to him. My sister Dominique's engagement, my brother Raoul's fervor for any movie with Belmondo in it, my crush on Karl Marx. We must have seemed like chattering children. Who would never quite grow up, as he already had. We could sort of tell he thought this.

As it happened, his visit was the last time the family was all together. Dominique married Étienne (not her best idea), and I left to go study at the Sorbonne. All this was hard on my mother, especially the absence of Yves, who had of course been her nicest child and the most attentive to her. She said she could never quite understand how someone like Yves couldn't find more time to visit his own family. She did not openly sulk, but we knew she felt ill-used.

And we hardly saw him in the next few years, we faded out of his view. When I went to his ordination, I was uncomfortable—we all were—at the sight of him in his cassock. During the ceremony, I felt confused and at the same time quite moved, as if a dog in a spangled costume had suddenly spoken profound and beautiful words.

In my life in Paris, I didn't mention Yves very often, but I wouldn't let anyone make jeering remarks about him, though I sometimes did myself. I was in my late twenties when I met Sylvie, and when we decided to have a wedding, it was clear that Yves should marry us. I had not been to Mass for years, but I closed my eyes when my brother placed the Host on my tongue, and I could hardly breathe from feeling all that I did.

And he toasted us at the reception too—"all my wishes for the truest happiness"—and he joked with my mother. He was working then in a shelter for homeless men in Marseille. My friend Bernard said Yves alone was enough to give the clergy a good name, after all those centuries of their being corrupt fat-cats or child-tormenting fascists. And it was true that Yves had taken on none of the slick manners some priests have—there were no sonorous depths in his voice—no, he was simply there, without ornament or strain. More than one person at the wedding said he seemed enviable, really.

It was less than a year after this that Yves left the priesthood. He sent us a letter to explain. "This decision has been a great anguish to me," he wrote. "I don't expect to cease mourning what I have given up. But I could not continue without hypocrisy and falsehood." It was clearly a letter he had sent not only to us. He had fallen in love with one Marguerite LaPorte, formerly Sister Ursule, and they had both chosen to go back into the world, as man and wife.

I should have been happy for him, but I was too startled at first. I had grown so used to thinking of him as someone beautifully suited to his calling. Now there was a scandal around him, a drama. I was perhaps more embarrassed than he was when he brought Marguerite to meet me and Sylvie in Paris. That bearded man was my brother—in a flannel shirt!—with his arm around a woman. She had a plain and lovely face, with pale eyes gleaming behind her spectacles, and thin brown hair cut short like a baby's.

We both liked her, how could we not? They went to live in Lille, where they worked at a center for teenage runaways, and in a year Marguerite gave birth to a boy, and she had a girl and another girl not very long after that, much to the delight of my mother. In the kitchen of our Paris apartment, Sylvie and I kept a photo of all of them walking in the rain, the baby girl in Yves's arms wearing his yellow rain hat.

Yves and his wife seemed utterly at ease as parents, unfazed by rowdiness, tickled by their kids' obsessions, and charmed by any bits of childish eloquence. My brother Raoul said, "See how healthy he is now, you can see it, no more of that flabby cadaver look." But any congratulations along these lines only caused Yves to shrug. I had read that there were married priests who still said the words of consecration at Mass, despite the rulings, and I asked Yves once if he ever imagined himself again at the altar, since, as these men said, he was ordained forever. He shook his head, more sadly than I could have expected, and said, "No, no. I knew. Every day I miss what I had. Every single day. But I can't have it, can I?"

I hadn't seen how terrible it was for him. When I told Sylvie this, she said maybe he would feel better as time went on, although a number of years had already passed. I did not tell my family what he'd said; they were so pleased that Yves's story had turned out to be a great romantic victory. Who knew what a romantic family I had? None of them would have understood his suffering, but later I thought that I did.

NO ONE EVER thought I was like Yves, certainly I didn't. I studied modern European history at the Sorbonne, and I was already out of school in 1968, loafing and working for a textbook publisher, when the student demonstrations broke into riots. Once I saw what was unfolding, I was in the streets too. I had long stopped being a Marxist, but I had, like the others, grown a purer scorn and a vaster ambition. I saw people clubbed on the back when we got boxed in on the Rue St. Jacques and the cops turned on us, lunging and hitting. We were all shouting, and my friend Bernard was bellowing howls of outrage—fury kept us from remembering to be afraid, which must be the secret of heroes.

I only saw bits and pieces of the actions. I had a job I went to—until the one-day general strike; I did march through Paris for that. We were all delirious that the workers had joined us. Bernard was glowing like a coal. *Already ten days of happiness,* the graffiti on the walls of the Sorbonne said. *Coming soon to this location: charming ruins.*

I suppose we had a month. I had a long argument with the editor I worked with, over whether the unions had sold out everyone by simply bargaining for higher pay. Only money! *No replastering,* the walls had said, *the structure is rotten.* I began with a biting rationality and escalated, in the face of the editor's suave derision, to a rant against those who lived only to consume. "Only morons think the world is all *things,*" I said. He had me fired, a nice irony in his defense of the workers.

It was the one time in my life I was fired for a principle, though all I really had was a contempt for unctuous compromise. I didn't starve either. I kicked around, writing translations of English tech manuals and tutoring *lycée* students who were afraid of flunking their *bacs.* I lived on this for quite a few years. I met Sylvie at a bistro so cheap the *frites* tasted of old scorched fat. She was a frugal student, eating alone before working all night on her thesis—I could guess this even before I started a conversation by complaining about the potatoes. "We're eating them anyway, aren't we?" she said. She was quite friendly for a woman that pretty.

"When potatoes first came to France," I said, "they banned them in Burgundy because they thought eating too many caused leprosy."

"Do I look spotted?" she said, holding out her arm.

"Not you," I said. I had a moment's pause after I said this, because Sylvie was black or North African or mixed—I couldn't quite tell and it was too soon to ask, but here we were, talking about her skin. She had smooth, sepia-toned arms. "Who do you think," I said, "brought potatoes back from Peru the way Marco Polo brought pasta from China?"

"Noodles were always everywhere. Nobody brought them," she said.

As it happened, Marco Polo was what she was writing about—he was her topic in Medieval and Renaissance Studies. I was a telepathic bumbler.

"He was sort of a liar, wasn't he?" I said.

"He was!" she said. "Once he was back in Venice, they called him *Il Milione*, the guy who told a million fibs. But he never budged. His famous line is, *I have not told the half of what I saw.* He said that on his deathbed, can you believe it?"

Her enchantment with him surprised me. Surely everyone had expected her to stay away from anything so Eurocentric. But I supposed her freedom was the point.

"Yes," she said. "Exactly."

I said I had meant to go further in history but hadn't liked the confinement of being a student. "Oh, it's prison, it's terrible," Sylvie said. But I could tell, as she spoke, that her own mental labor was a tonic to her—she loved to dig in, she loved to be reading so closely that the thirteenth century was under her eyelids. She was never not working.

But she liked my loose and shambling style, as it turned out. She was impressed at how easily I got by, how little worrying I did. I don't know why I was her emblem of successful insouciance. Lucky for me—it was sexier than just being nice.

WINNING SYLVIE ALWAYS dazzled me. And we lived for three years in my tiny, cluttered apartment in the 7th *arrondissement,* getting by on very little money, until Sylvie found that she was pregnant. Her father had once warned her that she might as well be living with a street juggler or a blind beggar as with me, the loafer. Sylvie's father was an insurance clerk from Meaux, a hearty man with tired blue eyes, and he had four daughters; I didn't blame him for wanting them well provided for. Her mother, who was from Guadeloupe, had fed me many delicious dinners on Sundays but had never been very interested in knowing me. All the same, they made their peace with the idea of me when they had to.

AND WE WERE very happy at our wedding. Sylvie in a dress like a column of light, me dazed and serious. The church in Meaux like a dark wooden ship, Yves's voice at the Mass. And then Sylvie's sisters moving through the reception, with their gold-dyed dreadlocks and their tightly combed chignons. My father leaned over to me, with his winey breath, and said, "Look at them. No girls could be lovelier. You know what? Soon the whole world will be like this."

"Not soon enough," I said, but I had not expected this from him and I was glad to hear him say it. It was my mother who was stiff and melancholy, greeting guests behind a thin smile. As teenagers Raoul and I once told her that a slave from Martinique was among the ancestors of Colette, her favorite writer, and she had refused to believe us—"I was never told that." "Dumas too," Raoul said. "A Haitian grandmother." My mother was doing her best now, she was trying as hard as she could (I thought, grimly). It was Yves who got her laughing and acting more amiable.

Sylvie's friends were teasing her about the hugely increased size of her breasts, a pleasant exaggeration on the friends' part. Sylvie was willowy and slender, and her pregnancy was still pretty concealed—but the friends were so detailed in their language that Sylvie, a generally dignified person, burst into fits of giggles. "Look at her now. All silly. What have you done to her?" her mother said to me, patting my arm. "You boy." When Sylvie and I left the reception, elated and drowsy, she kept calling me you boy.

EVEN BEFORE THE wedding, I had registered to take the exam for a secondary teaching diploma. Why shouldn't I teach the youth of the nation, how could it be any worse than the tutoring I already did? So I kept saying—though to pass the exam I had to remember all the tedious passages I had memorized under protest in my own fettered boyhood. My schooling had been hateful, my *lycée* run by cynical faculty who taunted the pupils into rote absorption and correct performance. Surely things had changed somewhat, yes? We spoke of my only having to do this until Sylvie had her degree and a university job, but I knew better even then.

And there was some satisfaction in cramming for the sake of my burgeoning family. I had my heroic labors, my nights of rigorous study. There is a lot to be said for sacrifice, particularly in its early stages. Those were not unhappy evenings, when I made soup for Sylvie and we sat at our separate desks. Sylvie was grateful for what I was doing, though she had to be careful in her words of praise; I was prickly, and sensitive to condescension.

When Marc was born, I was already teaching, and the students wrote words of congratulation on the chalkboard. Felicitations to me! I was teaching in the 13th *arrondissement,* which was just beginning to be an Asian enclave then, and one Chinese student gave me a potted tree in honor of a healthy boy. Right away Marc looked like Sylvie, with his pointed chin and his dandelion fuzz of hair—some nurses were surprised I was the father.

Those first sleepless months were too amazing for us to bear standing up. At home I was a crooning zombie walking Marc back and forth in the depths of the night in the hallways of our new apartment, or I was collapsed in bed, with the baby between us. At school I was hardly ever fully awake. Once I did start to fall asleep while I was listening to a student give a report—I got through it by making clownish wisecracks about my fatherhood.

LATER, WHEN YVES had his children, we'd watch all of them chasing each other like squirrels in his narrow backyard, and he and I would glance at one another—we liked to see them a little wild. And each of us was astonished, I think, at his own shimmering domestic contentment. The priest and the goof-off—who would have thought we would end up here? Sylvie and Marguerite liked to sit out by the rock garden in deck chairs and listen to Duke Ellington tapes, while we rolled around in the dirt with the kids. "The dog fathers," Sylvie said. It was all very jolly.

———

WHEN YVES'S OLDEST boy, Luc, was celebrating his eighth birthday, we drove up to Lille one Saturday at the beginning of October. It was a long, rainy trek in our rattletrap car, but Sylvie had just been told she'd been hired for a job she wanted at the Université, and she was in high spirits. When we got to the party she cornered Marguerite at once to tell her everything. I got dragged by Marc to an awning in the backyard, under which a group of children was admiring a goat. The goat belonged to Marguerite's sister Edmée, who had taken up organic goat farming and brought the nanny goat with her in a truck from Poitou, where she had a herd outside Surgeres. Yéyé, the goat, had a nice white face, with darkish splotches around her amber eyes and a dapper little forward-curling beard. Luc fed her carrots, and the others were allowed to pet her gently.

Edmée was a small, winsome woman with a spiky haircut—she didn't look to me like a farmer. She said she liked her work, though. "It's just complicated enough to be interesting," she said, "but there's no stupid boss or meetings or sucking up to anybody." I might have guessed this answer, but she made it convincing.

"Is there culture in the land of the goats?" I said. "Leaping dance recitals? Tailbrush art?"

"I go up to Paris quite often," she said. "Goaty though I may be."

I thought then of the pheromone research I'd read about in the news, which claimed that women's essential scent was fishy and men's was goaty. Thinking of it made me want to sniff myself. Meanwhile Edmée was showing Marc the dugs Yéyé gave milk from.

Later in the afternoon, one of the boys let the goat off her tether when no one was looking, and she went skipping off into the rain. I ran after her, out of family loyalty, and both Edmée and I ended up skidding down the rock garden in the mud. Scraped and wet, we got the creature back, but it took much tugging and hauling and slipping into the peony bushes. The kids loved it. In the kitchen Edmée wiped the mud off my face with a wet dish-cloth. "See! You're a goat too," she said. It was an odd moment.

AND SHE DID call me when she was in the city. I got a message at school, and I met her after work in a café. She looked up from the table, her face clearing at the sight of me, like any woman waiting for her date. *Her date.* I had time to think about what I was doing, but I did it anyway. "Thank you for coming," she said. I laughed, rolling my eyes. We had some chitchat about why none of my students liked Mitterand anymore—we were just talking to be talking—and then we went to her friend's apartment, while her friend was at work. I was so transfixed with arousal by this time that I had stopped worrying about anything, and Edmée was very simple and direct, but there was a tremulous undercurrent in her when I drew her against me.

The friend's bedroom was painted a pale, washy blue, to make it calm above what was really a very noisy street. When we first turned to each other on those white, white sheets, I felt that we were floating in a rush of sound. Then the noises faded out of my attention. Edmée was a slow and dreamy lover, and I tried to be careful with her, though I was lunatic with wanting. Even the subtler turns seemed to ravish her with feeling, and I wondered if she had not been with many men; she was close to thirty. But perhaps this was her only way of doing anything, this earnestness—she was so frank and transparent. Once I was actually inside her, I could not be slow, though she wept in passion (were those sobs?) long before we were near our finish. Or my finish, as it happened.

But I had made her happy, nonetheless. It did seem so. She lay with her head on my chest and said, "So nice, so nice." She did not want to be touched further, but she kissed my knee for a long time, as if I needed thanking. She said she had been thinking of me since the goat chase, and we sat up in bed holding hands, though I could not stay much longer.

EDMÉE FOUND REASONS to come to Paris as often as every two weeks, but she said she told her fellow farmers nothing. She would call me at school when she arrived, and I'd go to meet her at her friend's building; its stained marble frontage and khaki hallways became beloved spots to me. I never met the friend. The weather went from fall to winter, and in that drafty room Edmée and I swam toward each other on the swirled sheets, with the radiator in the corner rattling like applause.

"Every time I come back to the farm," she said, "Yéyé and the others can tell something very good has happened to me. They act differently. They run around in circles."

"They're goats," I said. "They're never sane."

"You don't know them," she said.

I let her tell me. They were highly resourceful animals, quite able to deceive and plot and play tricks. Most farms slaughtered the females by the time they were eight, but hers was going to let them live out their natural span of fifteen. I did not altogether see how someone like her had come to take such an interest, but she said that only showed my limit, my bookishness. She was always bringing me twigs and branches from the country—oak and beech and chestnut, which I examined and admired, bare and brown though they were. It pained her when I said I could not take them home with me.

She ran the goat operation with two women friends from school and two men who were a couple. The five of them were in each other's company more than they could like, and in that monotony Edmée had her loneliness. Once I gave her a Walkman radio with headphones—a waterproof one—that I thought she might wear while she was with the herd. I think she found it a useless and amusing present (what did I know about her chores?), but she crowed and threw her arms around me nonetheless. I really could do very little that displeased her.

IF SYLVIE GUESSED, she gave no sign. I didn't think she guessed. I never stayed later with Edmée than I meant to, or ate a meal with her, or saw her on the days I had to pick up Marc from school. Marc had become involved in a feud between factions of boys in his class, and Sylvie and I spent our suppers suggesting peace strategies to him, views more enlightened than he'd listen to. Sylvie and I were united in this. We had our conferences (while Marc did his homework) about whether race and skin color were factors in these schoolyard hostilities (he said no, but all his friends were from Algerian and Tunisian families) and whether the boys should be left to settle it themselves, a conclusion we reached together after much back-and-forth.

But at night in the bedroom with Sylvie, I must have seemed distant or depressed. When any caressing began between us, I could not follow through. I saw her beauty as I had always seen it, I was never anything but attracted to her, but I could not be a man who was intimate with two women's bodies. So it seemed. And Sylvie didn't ask me any questions or voice any accusations. She was too proud and probably unwilling to know. It was a kind of modesty in her, a prudence. When she saw I did not want coaxing in bed, she turned away but she kept her hand on my hip to remind me she was my friend.

AND EDMÉE WAS sadder each time we said goodbye to each other in that pale blue room. As I stood pulling on my pants, I saw her features blur and grow tearful and I thought, I've become a man who can't be bothered with a woman's weeping. I bent down and held her against me to comfort her, but what help was that when I was the cause?

There was no way for us to go on. Nothing but damage could come from it. Quite soon it became unbearable. I never told

Sylvie an outright lie, but I lied sometimes to Edmée, so she would not know I was going off to buy Sylvie a present or to meet her at her campus. I was becoming wily and hollow from pretense. And no one said anything, so perhaps I was good at it.

I went to Bernard's apartment and phoned Edmée in the country, and we had our talk. "So soon?" she said. "I thought we would have more time." While she was crying, she said that of course she had known I would stick to my marriage and my family (neither of us used Sylvie's name), my being that sort of man was what she had first admired in me. It was a terrible, sentimental conversation. Both of our voices broke the whole time. I praised her loveliness and her fineness, and everything I said sounded false, though it was true. We had to stop talking so that words could mean something again in our mouths.

I WAS NOT better after this either. For a while I was worse. I lived in torment as if I were still torn between two lovers; yet I did not really consider undoing my choice. But I might as well have been with Edmée all day. The flavor of her was in the Battle of Agincourt, she was folded into the Edict of Nantes, and the Tennis Court Oath had her scent in it. I liked teaching more than I had once expected to, but my days now seemed very long, and I could not always remember why I was standing in front of the room.

At home I slept a good deal, when I could. It was a terrible labor for me to lead a double life, and I wasn't even really leading it anymore. I didn't see how other people managed to move at all under the burdens of their duplicities—and perhaps they did have to work hard. The world was full of lies and disguises. I could tell how weary everyone was all around me.

IN AUGUST, Sylvie went away to Venice for three weeks, to read some crumbling records about the Polos for a book she hoped to write. Marco Polo had brought back a Tartar slave from Asia, whom he later freed in his will, and Sylvie wanted to see about him and about the market of foreign slaves in Venice. I stayed home with Marc, who was out playing with his friends most of the day, though he sometimes consented to walk around the empty August streets with me. Both of us slept late, a thing Sylvie always hated.

With Sylvie gone, I was afraid of the temptation to phone Edmée. I woke up every day at ten-thirty with this fear in the room like a fog. But the weeks of solitude had a different effect. I read books in the living room with the blinds drawn and ate my picnic lunch alone under a tree in the Jardin des Plantes, and then I went home again to our apartment, with its heavy quiet and its overgrown palms. I missed my wife.

And it was really Sylvie I missed, not some notion of her. When Sylvie arrived from the train station, I saw her in our door-way and I was wild with delight to have her in front of me, right there, still there. She was putting down all her luggage, unloop-ing it from her shoulders, and it seemed a miracle that she was doing this so that she might wrap herself around me. "Ouf," she said, pressed to my chest. "I think I must've been gone for decades, like the Polos."

"Too long," I said. Our son was hopping around like a rabbit.

She had brought him a gaudy souvenir gondola, black plastic splashed with gilt. Later she said to me, "I wish you'd been with me in Venice." She said this in bed, and it meant (I thought) that the gorgeous, encrusted, overladen beauty of Venice in the fetid August vapors—as she described it—had been so sexy as to wound her slightly without me. "Home is good too," I said, somewhat stupidly, but any tender statements between us had the right effect just then.

MY TIREDNESS DID not leave me, I saw that it might never leave, but Sylvie and I were companions to each other again. We debated what to do about Marc's balky homework habits, I came home with funny tales of what my students said about Napoleon. We were back to being lovers—back to the rewards of requited love—and back to being people who consulted each other on color matches in clothes or the meanings of current events.

Sylvie thrived in this stage, it seemed to me. For all that was unspoken between us, there was great relief in our house, a tacit gladness. And Sylvie at her ease was splendidly articulate, quite something to talk to. Her writing went well, refreshed by the flowing waters of our chatting and expounding and holding forth at home. Even Marc, who was becoming broody and picky, could not conceal his enchantment with his mother, and he still endured her kissing his face whenever she wanted. Almost whenever.

WE HAD TWO good years like this, and the sense to savor them. Sylvie was doing so well with her Polo project that she got ready to mount another research trip, this one much farther away. She wanted to go to Yangzhou in China, the city Marco Polo claimed he'd governed for the Khan for three years, though no Chinese record showed it. But communist workers in the 1950s had uncovered tombstones clearly identifying Italians who died in Yangzhou in the fourteenth century, maybe a community Polo had once led. Sylvie's only chance of seeing those tombstones was to wangle some sort of invitation from a Chinese university, and she made repeated visits to the embassy of the People's Republic, to guilds of Asian history scholars, and even to French Maoists, of which there were still a few. Marc was not pleased that she wanted to go anywhere and kept telling her she would have to eat fried locusts and drink snake wine if she went.

I didn't want her to go either. Even if I didn't think of Edmée so much anymore, I couldn't have said that she was absent from my mind. Why did Sylvie need to take herself away when we were doing so well? These times were precious. But I would have been ashamed to keep her from going where she wanted. I had never been that sort of husband.

Sylvie was dogged in her visits to the Chinese embassy. This single-mindedness was her one advantage, and she knew it.

When she wasn't back in time for supper one evening, Marc said, "Does she *enjoy* waiting in their hallway?" We were both irritated, hungry for dinner and tired of waiting for Sylvie to come home. It was the last night we had to be something as small and easy as irritated.

WHAT HAPPENED TO Sylvie never seemed likely to me. I had to be told more than once in the first call from the police; different people had to get on the phone to keep telling me. I couldn't get any of it to fit what I knew of the world. She walked down the steps of the Chinese embassy and the earth cracked in two and swallowed her up. It was not the first bomb to go off in Paris—there were others in those years, in a shopping center, in an art gallery, in a bookstore—set by pro-Iranian or North African groups. Perhaps this particular blast of death was a mistake, not meant to explode where it did. Marc clung especially to the idea that someone killed his mother *by mistake*. I heard him say that to his cousins; I think he was attached to this irony, in those first days. For myself, I wanted to think that the bomb had gone off in an instant, that Sylvie was walking down the steps, thinking dreamily of Yangzhou and its network of canals and stone bridges, and her life was over before she had time to be afraid.

LATER, A FRENCH official told me the explosive could have been placed by Uighurs, a Turkic Muslim group who lived in China's northwest (Marco Polo met them). But no one ever claimed Sylvie's bomb. So perhaps it didn't achieve its purpose. This was not so long after Lockerbie either. When she first heard what had happened, Sylvie's mother said, in her tears, "The whole world's going to blow up. That's what they want. It's going to be nothing. Now that it's all tied together."

The city of Paris was hideous that week, with its spring rains and its bleary lights and its honking noises and Sylvie dissolved into the watery dimness. No place could have been more enraging to walk in. I knew that Marc felt this too. And we couldn't finish any task without being stopped by a friend's phone call or a journalist's knock or our own lapses into vacancy. Everything interrupted us, and this sense of intolerable interruption had to do (we came to realize) with being cut off from Sylvie. We were still in mid-sentence. I especially had not said half of what I meant. And Sylvie, as everyone pointed out, wasn't going to get to China, or write the rest of her book, or watch Marc leave childhood.

S O M E   O F   M Y students came to the funeral. It pleased me to see them there, dressed up and solemn in the church. Their expressions were so changed I almost didn't recognize a few, in their suits and slicked-down hair. I wanted to ask the Chinese kids (who had probably never been Buddhists) or the Cambodians (who probably still were) what they thought about reincarnation. I was interested now in the notion that Sylvie's lifetime

wasn't meant to be complete in itself. Naturally, she hadn't finished—how could she have? (Unlike my son, I didn't want the
whole thing to be a mistake.)

The priest who was my mother's cousin came from Lyon to offi-
ciate at the funeral. I took Communion with the others, but I
didn't pray for Sylvie, not that week and not later. I was so horrified at the half-lies in the last years of our marriage, I had a great
dread of tainting my mourning with falsity. I didn't go again to
church. I wanted to honor Sylvie by as strict an honesty as I could
practice. Perhaps it was backwards of me to be so scrupulous now.
Yves was disappointed—not even lighting a candle? not saying any
prayers at home?—however, being Yves, he said I should do as I felt.

Marguerite told me she was praying every day for whoever set
the bomb. Marc, on the other hand, said he hoped the murderer
fried in hell. He was only thirteen, and half the people I knew
said the same thing in some way (I didn't). "We don't even know
who did it," I said.

"*I* know," he said. "A Muslim, right?"

"No one knows that," I said.

On Marc's first day back at school, he came home complaining the place was overrun with apes, he could hardly sit at his
desk without puking. Wasn't he glad to see his friends? "What
friends?" he said. His classmates Malik and Abdallah had been at
the funeral. He said they gave him the creeps, he wasn't talking
to them now. "Apes," he said.

At the end of the first week he came home bruised and dirty
and I could see he'd been fighting.

"Not this," I said, "please."

He hadn't let his old friends walk with him, he'd pushed them when they came near him. "It's my own business," he said.

Sylvie could have talked to him. He might have listened to her, his favorite parent and the one whose looks he carried, on these delicate matters of hate. "You *can't* be like this," I said. "Do you understand that? Do you know who we are?"

"Don't yell at me." He was weeping, in the midst of his sullenness. I needed Sylvie very badly to help me with this.

"Where will this lead?" I said.

"Nowhere," he said.

He wouldn't talk any more to me, not about the fight or about anything. And he didn't want to go to school the next day. I let him stay home while I was at work—he could sleep or watch videos or whatever he wanted—but we couldn't do that forever.

I sent him to Lille to stay with Yves and Marguerite before anything worse happened. Just for a few months. I didn't know what else to do.

HE SEEMED RELIEVED to go. But then I was truly by myself, and the apartment was a box of bare rooms. I kept seeing Sylvie out of the corner of my eye. When I was out walking in the street, I would catch her shape within the other shapes of the world, like a figure in a puzzle. *Sylvie.* Then I would remember and feel foolish, like a dog leaping for a stick no one has thrown. I saw why people believed in ghosts. Though I did not.

My friend Bernard telephoned me every few days, and in the evening he came to take me out to hear jazz in clubs, a thing we hadn't done since our twenties. I hated, with fresh indignation, the affectations of everyone sitting near us in those clubs—smoking, leaning toward each other, self-satisfied and imbecilic. But I was grateful for the music, when it was any good. It gave me a solace without language, the only kind I could stand. Bernard had a favorite trumpet player, an American he thought sounded like an updated Chet Baker, doleful and cool. His trumpet had a weary playfulness, slipping into sly turns and thoughtful pauses—just right, we thought. "Andre!" Bernard would shout. "More of that, please! We beg you!" Andre would give the shyest of bows.

I would not say I enjoyed myself in those clubs but these were moments when I was not suffering. But often I wouldn't go, I couldn't stand being around people. I had lost my tolerance for ordinary conversation; the most harmless exchange of everyday insincerities kept appalling me. Who did I think I was? If I stayed in and kept myself away from all lying, from my own lies and from everyone's, what did that prove?

Marc called from Lille every night. His conversation was already more innocent, from being with his younger cousins. He had fished in a pond and run races up and down the pasture when the kids went to visit their Aunt Edmée in the country. Edmée had left the goat farm and was living with a veterinarian. They had horses, Marc said, had I ever been on a horse? He had been on one of their horses, Hubert the black one, an extremely smart animal.

For almost three years, part of my mind had been dreaming always of Edmée. Were those years misspent? What was the point of all that longing? I supposed I was glad she had found a man to be with, though gladness was not my first feeling. How fascinated I had once been, watching her over and over in the cinema of my brain. What was the point of all that longing?

I had a week left of school before the summer vacation, and on Friday I stayed in my classroom grading papers for hours, and then I went out into the balmy blue evening. On the corner by the news kiosk I saw Sylvie in a coral-red shirt, just a glimpse. It wasn't Sylvie; I knew that. Was I going to be haunted all my life? When I first met Sylvie and I was smitten with constant desire, I used to walk around reminiscing about the night before, recalling her as vividly as anything actually before me in the world. But that haunting had had no sting to it; it had only been celebratory, a basking in retained heat.

On the way to find something to eat, I passed a storefront temple with a slender golden Buddha sitting in it. A Cambodian place, as far as I could guess from the writing. The Buddha looked quite settled on his lotus, with his hands curved in his lap. Stiff but poised. *He* wasn't longing for anything, I knew that much. He'd cast aside his ego (whatever that was) a while ago. And he'd said anyone could do this, which I could hardly believe. Though people in a large part of the world did believe it.

Well, I thought on the way home, what would be left without longing? It gave me something to ponder, something new at least, while I was buying my bachelor meal of *charcuterie* and bread and grapes and walking into my empty house. I forgot about it while I ate and watched the news on TV. But I didn't forget. Before I went to bed, I got out a book on Asian religion I'd had since college and read around in it. So what *would* be left? Everything just the same, nothing special, various sages had apparently said, in their cool and shrugging way. But without fear or clinging. This last phrase, from a Theravadan commentator, did sink into me.

All weekend I kept sneaking back to the book, though it often put me to sleep. But how radical it was. I'd had no idea. The self is a delusion—millions believed this? I was a tourist in these neighborhoods, a rube scratching his head, but I had the traveler's reward of an opened imagination.

On Monday, on the way home from school, I stopped in at a bookstore and bought another book, this one written by an American who'd been a monk in Thailand. And in the night, when I couldn't sleep, that was what I read. I found comfort in the flavor of it, even if I did not exactly swallow it whole. I told no one what I was reading, so I would not have to exaggerate my agreement or talk it down either. It was my secret habit.

So that was what I did in the two months while Marc was away. I listened to music and I soaked myself in paragraphs that had the exquisite preposterousness of possible accuracy. Part of me waited for Sylvie to come back. Every day I had to remind myself not to wait.

———

MARC MUST HAVE been waiting too, at Yves's in Lille. When he came home in August, he had grown taller in a way that made his head look small on his body. When I asked if he still hated people who happened to be Muslims, he seemed surprised—and disgusted with me for posing such a question. "It's a *religion*," he said.

"You're not going to fight anymore?"

"*No,*" he said. "I can't believe you're even asking."

I was afraid of outbreaks of revenge from the others, but in school the kids who had once been his friends left him alone, and he kept to himself, for the most part. Every so often he brought home one of the squeaky, round-faced boys in his class who were the furthest from puberty, and they played endless board games, games Marc had liked when he was younger. He'd call me over to watch them. He had decided to be younger. He nagged me to go to the park with him, he was impatient when I was on the phone. I had to get used to his hovering. At night we sat on the sofa, watching Lucky Luke and Jolly Jumper cartoon videos together. At least we had our own pocket of privacy, our living room as a retreat from the maelstrom of whatever Paris was doing outside. When a bomb exploded aboard a French plane in Niger, I didn't tell Marc about it; why should I? He already didn't feel safe, and both of us had had enough of history. I was doing my best not to think about anything beyond what to make for supper and where Marc had lost his sweater. I didn't want to hear about someone else's bloody outrage over some murderous stupidity in the past.

This was an odd state of mind for someone who taught history for a living and went forth every day to explain to sixteen-year-olds why they should care about the Hundred Years War. My student Xing Yao wrote, "The war was caused by greed over Flemish wool. Joan of Arc was not greedy, however. She rode a spooky white horse and heard the dangerous voices of ghosts. The English had to burn her to get rid of the ghosts."

When I read this paper and was stumped over what to correct, it struck me that it was probably very much like what Marco Polo had written about China. He saw it his way. Polo didn't mention bound feet or calligraphy or the Great Wall—proof, many scholars thought, that he was never in China—and no Chinese had bothered to record any Polo serving as an official in Yangzhou. But I thought that each side might simply have been caught up in noticing what it wanted to.

I had a new feeling for Marco Polo's dislocation, since I was now a wanderer in the bleached and trackless deserts of mourning. Sylvie would have been interested in this feeling. No one else would care—I had a gush of self-pity, for all my unaired thoughts. Years of them stretched ahead.

On a Saturday afternoon when Marc was at soccer practice, I went to the Cloud Mountain Chan Buddhist Center near my school to learn how to meditate. It was the one unfalse thing I could think of doing to help myself, and an excitement rose in me as I went into the room, which was in the back of a Chinese bookstore. If this gave me any relief at all, I was going to be very grateful. People were sitting cross-legged on squares of foam rubber—plenty of French people as well as Asians—and a young Chinese woman smiled and gestured for me to take a chair in the back. How sweet she was. A thin elderly man with black-framed glasses gave the instructions in Chinese and a boy in jeans translated them into French. I might have gone to a more European group, but I liked this. The meditation guidelines were familiar from my reading, and I was suddenly very sure that it was all going to be very easy, like resting on buoyant air.

When the gong sounded, I was enormously pleased to be there. I counted each breath in and out, I tried to have no thoughts at all. Why hadn't I come before? To be acutely conscious but free of my grasping, chattering self was a glorious project. I could not do it for more than about ten seconds. I supposed I had been warned of its difficulty. Who can think about not thinking? I began again, over and over. But I did not expect what happened. While the other beings in the room breathed softly and evenly, I was close to moaning aloud because I could not stop remembering that Sylvie was ashes. In this room of breathing strangers, I was seething with humiliation, to think that my wife had been murdered while I was lying on a pile of cushions at home, reading about a soccer match. As if I had been forced to watch her blown to bits, while I ate an apple, an idiot on a sofa. To be here now with this fuming in me, surrounded by rows of silent people who did not have to bear it, was insufferable. I despised all of them—why were they making me stay?— and I could not wait until the gong sounded, though I did wait.

I stayed for the Dharma talk too, because no one else left;

what a fraud I was. I got away finally as people were passing out tea and cakes—they were a perfectly kind group—and I was never doing anything like this again. I went home so heavy with disappointment that I could barely make my way down the steps of the Métro. I hadn't needed one more thing to fail me.

MARC CAME HOME saying, "Soccer is a stupid game," which meant he'd had a bad day. In the kitchen he peeled the fruit while I made our routine weekend meal of *boudin* cooked with apples. I had enough to do, didn't I, just watching over him. He was not difficult these days but he was too quiet. My sister Dominique, whose own teenagers were shoplifters and fire-setters, said he'd become like a nice dog you didn't notice. After dinner he and I started to put together a castle out of a kit; it was a model of the Château de Chambord, with seventy-seven wooden parts. I tried not to worry about what Marc was going to do when he had to be more than thirteen.

It took days to finish the castle and then Marc surprised me by giving it to Clotilde, Sylvie's mother. He said she liked elegant things, which was true. Her face lit up at the gift; I had rarely seen her that delighted, and certainly not in recent months. I wondered then if he was going to be like Yves.

Marc had certain traits of Yves's—a taste for ridiculously detailed projects like the castle, a resistance to other kids' opinions, a niceness with his older relatives. What did this mean? In Lille Marc had gone to Mass with his cousins, but when I asked if he wanted to go in Paris, he said, "Are you nuts?" If he had a streak of piety, it was going to surface outside the family's legacy.

As perhaps mine was, my streak. My thirst. In my sleepless nights I had begun to read certain books again, those explanatory texts that tried to bring the Dharma to the postmodern European reader. I had the imprecise but lasting sense that they were doing me good. The writers could not stop talking about *impermanence*. And its relentless presence in every single thing (why was this news?) gave me less reason to feel my own loss as exceptional. It was a help to me to feel that Sylvie consumed in flame was not exceptional, though I could not have told anyone why. It saved me from a kind of vanity.

As Marc grew older, he had Yves's thin neck and square, stiff shoulders, and his hair was in the same limply short cut favored by gawky boys thirty years before. His physique underwent hormonal changes with a determined neutrality; he looked like a child but with a man's voice and body hair. He spent many of his waking hours in computer games. Girls liked him, as time went on—they phoned him with gossip about cliques and pleas for advice. What ruses girls had to resort to. He talked to them for hours, so he could not have been annoyed at their phone calls. A few of the boys he knew were already sexually active, but he was waiting, I could see, to step into any sort of drama. I hoped not waiting forever.

BERNARD SOMETIMES ASKED if I didn't want to start seeing a woman sometime. I didn't. When we were in clubs, listening to an alto sax move around a familiar tune, I'd remember the lyrics—*mon dieu, mon dieu, mon dieu, laissez-le-moi encore un peu, mon amoureux*—and they seemed demented, like lines a figure from Marc's space-aliens game might shriek, sheer blaring urgency. In the smoky darkness, I glanced at the profiles of women at nearby tables, their slender, soft bodies tucked casually into their clothes, and their femaleness was admirable and extreme and too raw to me.

I WAS MARC'S chief companion in these years. We'd watch the TV news and invent scripts of the announcers' real thoughts (they tended to fixate on their bodily functions), and Marc did a clumsy but really quite funny imitation of Jacques Chirac. We were beside ourselves one night over an interview with an aging actor who was wearing what seemed to be a satin jumpsuit. An ego positively gets in your way as you get older, I thought, watching the actor flip back his shock of hair. "An Elvis *manqué*," Marc said. At least he didn't say anything like that about me. For the most part, I wasn't giving him a florid repertoire of pretenses to point out.

Sometimes in the evenings I took myself out to hear talks by a very famous Vietnamese monk with a settlement near Bordeaux or a Parisian from a Zen order brought to France by a missionary Japanese monk in the sixties. When I came home from these talks, Marc would be asleep in his room in front of the computer, his cheek on his desk. I'd wake him, and if he swore he'd finished his homework, we'd grill demi-baguettes stuffed with Nutella in the sandwich press, Marc's favorite snack. I loved those ends of the night—my head still aerated from the talks and Marc babbling about Nintendo and the two of us bent over the comradely mess of oozing chocolate.

Past midnight on one of these nights, I was in bed in my room when I was awakened by what seemed to be the noises of sex, muffled gasps and sighing groans. Could Marc have someone with him? My own sweet boy, what secrets he kept. But the cries, I soon knew, were from the floor above me, the bedroom of a twenty-year-old girl who worked in a bank and lived at home. Marianne must have smuggled in a lover while her family was out. I wasn't sure I wanted to overhear the pleading whimpers of a girl I saw every day in the hallway. But I was amused too. Oh, good for her. I thought they'd better hurry up before her parents walked in, and they did seem to be picking up speed. I could tell they were trying, without much success, to be quiet too. How cute that was, their inept stealth.

They went on just a while longer—the raised volume of their last stages must have been what had broken my sleep. When they were silent, it occurred to me that all this sex pulsing through the ceiling had not made me think of Sylvie, and so I remembered her then, the lost sensations of her, and I thought of Edmée too. But listening to the couple's cries had not made feel me lonely, though I had much to be lonely about. Or even left out. Why hadn't it? Instead I had been amused. I had become someone who was amused by these things. As if my own long story was just another story.

———

IT WAS AN interesting feeling, that amusement, and I had it at other times during these years. It might have come to me naturally, but I gave the Buddha credit. Once when I was signing up for auto insurance, I told the woman at the desk "deceased" when she asked "spouse's name," and she gasped and said, "I'm so sorry. Excuse me. So sorry." And I thought—the world is full of husbands whose wives are gone. She's been at her desk so long the news hasn't reached her. I had to joke with her about my birth date to lighten things up, but I was already light. Or once when I was teaching my class, the students were arguing about the Baader-Meinhof Gang, and one of the boys said, "I admire the beauty of their convictions and to blow people up is not the worst evil," and there was a sudden silence. The students all knew about my wife. I was the only person in the room who was free of wretched embarrassment. I led them back to some earlier line of debate (could the cruelties of capitalism be checked by threats? more readily thirty years ago or now?) but even the defiant ones were still fidgety and dumbstruck. So I talked, my breath an easy wind we all floated on.

———

MARC STAYED WITH me, even after he had passed his matriculation exams. He continued to live at home while he studied computer engineering and looked, to the rest of the world, like a man. Over the years, I had learned not to make inquiries about girls, the one thing that led him to outbursts of hostile wrath. I didn't care if he liked boys instead, but that was not a remark he liked either.

But once he'd started going to the engineering institute, I heard him mention, without scorn, the names of people in his classes. Mathieu, Benoît, Victoire, François, Catherine. I came home from work one day to find a mixed group of three in the living room—a plump girl with huge earrings, a lanky boy with bleached hair, a bearded guy in a suit—listening to Afro-pop at top volume. They chatted politely with me; they were nice enough kids, but I had a strong urge to leave the apartment when they were there, an impulse they were delighted to see me indulge.

And it was only a few months after this that Marc moved in with Catherine, the plump girl (who looked a bit like one of Sylvie's sisters). They were not a couple, he told me—did people always have to be couples? Catherine lived in an apartment with many small rooms, on a run-down, lively street near the Gare de l'Est, not far from where I was taking a yoga class. I used to stop in to visit them on my way home, and I liked seeing Marc at his ease on Catherine's lipstick-red armchair, his feet up on the matching ottoman, sipping her cups of hot chocolate. "Your father looks so young," Catherine said. "You should try yoga too, you're so lazy."

"My father is a monk *manqué*. He has unusual patience," Marc said. "I'm already too great to need any exercise. A fitter version would be too much for the world."

Catherine snickered. They got along very well, whatever they were doing.

I LIKED THE yoga and I wasn't bad at it either. But I wasn't used to being so near my body parts, stretching my nose to my knee or holding my buttocks in my hands to thrust my legs over my shoulders. The class was mostly women, of various ages, twisting next to me on the foam rubber mats as we shifted and reached and held our poses. The teacher, a Belgian woman who had taken an Indian name, would place her hand on my back or abdomen to correct me, and the contact always startled me; out of nowhere, the gentle flat of her palm.

My balance was not bad and I could hold a shoulder stand for what I considered a valiant length of time. The pose felt like reverse flight, my feet pointing upwards to the celestial ceiling. One morning a woman in front of me teetered and almost fell on me, feet first. I whispered my forgiveness upside down, while she righted herself. She was the class's voluptuous American, a woman close to my age with a figure like Brigitte Bardot, icon of my boyhood—what riches was heaven showering on me? I had to laugh. I kept her giggling too, even after we were sitting again. She reacted well to silliness. Her French was good.

There was no harm, I thought, in asking her to lunch. I was not surprised when she said yes—she was so bouncy and agreeable and American. But there was something smudged and sad about her, and I discovered at lunch that her marriage had ended not long before. "He wasn't a cad," she said. "People seem to want me to say that now. But I don't."

I thought most Frenchwomen would have found something more biting to say.

"Yes, well, I didn't become French—my husband's family would tell you that. I'm still a bad cook too. Can you believe it? But when I go home, they'll think I'm a kitchen genius."

She was on her way home to the U.S., would be gone very soon. She would miss, she said, the good butter and the real tomatoes and the *céleri-rave en rémoulade*. She ate with childish gusto.

"Well, don't go then," I said. She smiled wanly.

What was she going home to?

"Perhaps I'll found a school of French yoga. Americans will think that's very sexy. They think everything French is sexy."

"Well, it is," I said. How roguish I was acting, all of a sudden.

A man came into the restaurant with a dog, a large Alsatian shepherd we both petted as it went by. "At home I'll have a dog," she said.

She sounded forlorn then. She pushed her straight, pale hair off her face as we watched the dog settle under the table. She was an old style of woman, tenderhearted and naïve in that opulent body, an answer to a dream I hadn't had.

I SAW THAT I was going to have to act quickly. Whatever we were doing we had to do soon, before she left. When I phoned her that evening, she was in her hotel room, reading, she said, a detective novel set in Miami, where she had once lived. I took her out to a film, a comedy about clever workers and a duped boss that we both liked. I sat in the darkened theatre, with more feeling in me than I needed (I thought), stunned to be seated again as a couple.

"That movie was so much fun, thank you so much, I needed fun," she said.

At the end of the night, in front of her crummy hotel, I leaned toward her. I was old to be at an angle of public uncertainty about a woman, old to be kissing anyone on the street. But it was a real kiss, or turned into one—I had not forgotten how to swim in these waters—and the bright shock of it had its own authority.

ALICE (THAT WAS HER NAME) talked a good deal about the U.S. but it was clear to me she had no plans. If she went to Miami, she could hardly be a showgirl again, as she had once been. Sometimes she waxed sentimental, telling me about the brilliant surf on Miami Beach or a fabled production of *The Wiz* she had seen on Broadway. Her mother's coconut cream pie or her great-aunt's hydrangeas. Though she had avoided her family for decades.

On the fourth night we became lovers. She came back to the apartment and we sat on the sofa drinking *pastis* and then we slipped into my bedroom without any difficulty. There was no shyness in her, but all her art (she was distinctly artful) was in the languorous aptness of her responses; I could feel her listening for me at every turn. I felt like an aging virgin, too long without sex (as she must have known), a gangling old puppy. But I thought Alice herself was moved by my swooning at her touch, and the poetry of lust sustained us through all the precipitous stages—the removal of our clothing, the lengthy exploration of intimate landscapes, the natural violence of the act itself.

In the moments when I could think, I was full of jubilation to find myself once again in the garden of earthly delights. Here again! Not too late! But I began to see that I was not quite in a terrain where I had ever been before. I was arrived from a long journey through ashes, I was the ragged wanderer stepping out from the dark wood. Now every sensation weighed on me more tenderly. For all that I hardly knew Alice, I was her serious lover.

ALICE WAS A little giddy afterwards. I had used a condom (after lecturing Marc for years about them) and she teased me about whether I had gone shopping and put in a good supply. I had, actually. It pleased her enormously to hear this. And then she put her head on my chest, kissed my nipple, and fell asleep. I had expected more conversation, and I lay awake, in some disappointment, but I was rapturous too. I drifted on astonishment.

She would not eat anything I had in the house for breakfast—she only liked American cold cereal in the morning. She looked clear and awake, her light hair shining under the kitchen light. She had gotten up with me at six-thirty, when I had to get ready for school.

"This is so cozy, your kitchen," she said.

"Small, you mean," I said.

"The best kitchen I ever had," she said, "was when I was in Miami. We had a big apartment, with a picture window and palm trees outside."

I thought how her face must have been when she was younger. She was like a faded doll now.

"The man I lived with broke the window when he was drunk.

He threw a chair through it when he was angry about something."

"Was he dangerous?"

"Not to me," she said. "Or we never got to that point. He was fine when he wasn't drunk. Alcohol was his demon. *A crying shame* is how I'd put it in English."

She had a lovely sort of wistful kindness, quite unusual.

And she refused my coffee. She was going back to bed again, if I didn't mind, and then she was going to walk around, just following her nose, seeing all the things she hadn't seen when she was living in the provinces. Who knew if she'd ever have a chance to see them again? She was too lazy to follow a map. She liked to amble, she hated to worry. That was how she was.

AS FAR AS I could see, the important thing was to make use of what time we had. Later in the week, I pointed out the waste in her paying money for the hotel, since she had stopped spending nights there anyway. I thought she could stay in France longer if she could make her francs last. Was she in a hurry to get home?

Not yet. She gave me a sunny look. And every day while I was at school, she did her eccentric sightseeing; she went to Baroque churches (the more fanciful the better) and designers' shops (just for looking) and every single bridge on the Seine (she loved bridges). At night we stayed in. We were in bed a good deal of the time. We seemed to be embarked on a kind of work together, an erotic project carried out with painstaking elaboration. Certain inventions had to be taken as far as possible. Certain gestures had be played out, ornamented and altered and branched into dizzying constructions. I thought it was my age that made the pointlessness of fear so clear to me, but it was probably Alice.

When I was in my twenties, an American woman I picked up hitchhiking told me, "French men think they're God's gift." I had never heard this expression in English and later could not resist repeating it to Yves, who was still a priest (he laughed). She was a sour, skinny girl from Chicago named Peggy, and I turned on the radio in the car (she hated Françoise Hardy too) to escape more discussion. But now her phrase floated up in my mind, and I thought of myself and Alice: guests at a banquet, lavished with manna. We did not thank each other directly—that would have been too meek and cloying—but beneath the abundance that exhausted us, we were, I think, both secretly humbled.

I TRIED NOT to worry about Alice leaving. She missed her parents, who had never come to visit. She missed hot dogs, American disc jockeys, and a lake in Wisconsin where her cousins used to summer. Bernard said to me, "There aren't really very many permanent expatriates. People usually do go home eventually, people like her."

It gave me such anguish when he said this that I walked for an hour in the rain, morose and sodden and too restless to take the Métro. Hadn't I been through enough? I could not help feeling sorry for my old, battered self; I was depressed and soaked when I reached my apartment. And there was Alice—calling out from the hallway, "Giles! You're home!"—glowing and glad to see me. What was I complaining about? When I hugged her, she was beautifully solid flesh. It was my own doing if I could feel her absence in my arms.

At dinner we had a small spat over why she always left the carton of cream out to sour. In her own country, I said, people probably didn't bother much about spoilage. Her voice was deep and coarse when she defended herself. Had I been longing for someone who wasn't there? What did I want?

I wanted it anyway. Later, when we were lying in bed after making love, I fell into dread again over how soon she was going to leave—perhaps before the end of the month, when the airline rates went up for summer—and then she'd be gone without a trace. That would be the end of it. Meanwhile Alice, in her actual corporeal form, lay nestling next to me.

ON MY WAY to school one morning, I passed the storefront temple with the golden Buddha seated in the same spot on his lotus blossom. I had grown to know him better, from my reading; his pronouncements had colored my thought. This particular statue, with his hands carefully placed in the meditation pose, sent a strict, no-nonsense calm out into the street. I had passed this figure for years with the sense that the two of us had a private life together. Our golden hours. Often I had a secret impulse to put my palms together and bow before him, as the Cambodians of the district did when they entered the temple. To see him in the glinting April light this morning made me remember (as if it were long ago, which it wasn't) the nourishment of my long nights of reading—not a lot of reading going on now—and the comfort of my intentions.

Goodbye to all that. I walked by him full of regret that I had slipped from my steadiness. *He* didn't care whether I had a lover or not—he was not opposed to these things, not exactly—but I had stopped needing him. I had used him and let him go. I hardly struggled anymore with his ideas. What was wrong with me that I couldn't keep two kinds of attention in my head at once? I skulked past the Buddha, homesick for what I'd left behind. I had not thought such a thing would be painful.

MARC SAID, "God, you look so much better than you used to. You used to look *gray*. Now you're a ruddy old personage."

Marc was a great fan of Alice. (Everyone said this was surprising in a son.) She adored the music on the CDs he played for us when we went there for supper—*zouk* from the French Antilles, zippy and fluid—and she let Catherine lead her in a few dance steps. Marc and I did not dance, but the women enjoyed themselves greatly. Marc said later, "She's very free but not vulgar," a compliment I did not repeat because it sounded too patronizing, too French, though it had real admiration in it. On another evening, when she wrenched open a stuck window in his kitchen—she really was very strong—he could not stop marveling at her athleticism. Catherine got her listening to the Caribbean radio station, so my apartment was filled with gently blaring brass and lilting vocals.

It was also littered with magazines and Alice's clothing. Alice was a carnival of abandoned objects. Sometimes she had fits of straightening up—she tried to clean the living room and drowned a favorite book of mine in spilled coffee, an old leatherbound edition of Montaigne.

"You loved that book," Alice said. "I feel terrible. Did you buy it at one the bookstalls by the river?"

"Yes," I said. Actually, it was an anniversary present from Sylvie.

Sylvie was not a secret, of course, but I did lie sometimes to save myself the difficulty of talking about her to Alice. I did this without thinking. I, who had wanted nothing so much as an honest life, was back to evasions and cover-ups. Some of these lies were forms of tact—I told Alice I enjoyed the games of honeymoon bridge she was so fond of playing. And some were flat denials of fact—I told her, for some reason, that I had always been faithful to my wife. I displayed a modest reluctance to brag about this. Yes, always. It seemed I could not be at close quarters with a woman I loved without staining myself with lies.

And Alice too sometimes twisted the truth, I came to see. She had not studied nearly as much ballet as her earlier reports suggested. Her husband might have been wildly crazy about her, but he was the one who had ended the marriage. In Paris one day she walked for miles all the way to the Bois de Boulogne but she also took a bus in between. There must have been other half-truths I had no way to guess.

When Alice's money was almost gone, she got the idea that she might teach some classes at the yoga center—I didn't expect her to be hired, but she was. So she wasn't going home that soon, despite what she said. She took me out to dinner to celebrate her first influx of cash, and we got drunk at the brasserie on the corner where I used to take Marc every Friday night. The owner did a corny waltz when he brought us the second bottle. Alice got up and danced a few measures with him, pleased as could be. I was embarrassed (what movie was this from? not one I liked) but I didn't mind very much. I was long past minding anything, I was like a macerated fruit soaked in happiness.

I HAD AN easy life, those first few years with Alice. When does anyone ever get to say such a thing? I did say it, to people who made the least inquiry about how I was. Who knew better than I did what was easy and what was not? Alice was no trouble. Her slackness and her untidiness and her love of aimless wandering were the loose ends of a generous nature. My home was a cushion of no-trouble.

We were just past the early, more exhilarated years, when I woke up in the middle of the night with a feeling as if a book had been slammed shut around something in my chest. Maybe I had simply eaten something, but it was not like anything I had eaten before. I lay rigid in fear while I waited to see what the pang in my chest was going to do. I thought about what Sylvie must have felt before she died. I was always thinking of Sylvie, I had never stopped thinking of her. She lived under my skin like a hidden layer of tissue. I felt now as if I could just almost speak to her, I wanted to speak. My heart was bursting with what I needed to say, I was on the edge of conversation.

The pang lifted, and when it didn't return, as the minutes went by, I could see that I was all right. I would have liked to tell Sylvie that I was okay after all. I should have told her not to go to the embassy—any fool in this century knew embassies were dangerous. Why didn't I ever try to talk her out of going? The Chinese only kept refusing her anyway. Meanwhile, Alice lay in bed next to me, in her eyelet nightgown, with her arm flung across her forehead, in a deep and oblivious slumber. Her hair still smelled of the American chicken she had fried for supper. Had this part of my life been a lie all along too?

I had to talk myself down from the horror of this question. It was no good asking it. I loved Alice. Sylvie was dead. End of story. How could they be vying for the same spot, when one of them no longer took up space?

ALICE, WHO WAS really quite superstitious, had a startling reaction when I told her I'd had a chest pain in the night that was really nothing. She went out to pray. There was no religion she'd been raised in or belonged to, but she walked into her favorite church, the Église du Dôme, of all places, and knelt for a while, hoping and requesting, and she lit a candle. It moved me to hear that she had done this for me. Where had the thought come from? I was by this time more Buddhist than Catholic, and had been going again to a Soto Zen center near my school, as she knew. She had probably loved the staginess of the great stone church, but I was moved nonetheless.

"She prayed near Napoleon's tomb?" Marc said, when I told him the story.

"Don't make fun of her," I said.

"It's a pompous church," Catherine said. "But Luc loves it too."

Yves' oldest son was getting his doctorate in architectural history. "Get Luc to take you on a tour of Invalides," Marc said. "He's actually not boring."

"Luc is smart," I said.

"Can you imagine if there were no Luc?" Catherine said. "Imagine if Marc's uncle had stayed celibate forever."

"Everybody thought he was going to," I said.

"I don't get it. How did Yves ever do it?" Marc said. "It makes no sense to me that people do that."

"Yves didn't mind so much," I said. "For a long time he didn't."

———

I THOUGHT THAT night about when Yves was young, when he first went into the Church. All my friends wanted to know if a girl had jilted him, was that the reason? Perhaps a girl had, but I didn't know about it. And perhaps later the Church jilted him, let him down with its arid institutional cruelty, and so he had been drawn to Marguerite. I could see that sex and religion were always fighting over the same ground—both with their sweeping claims, their promises of transport—and each ran into the breach left by the other, each tried to fill in for the other's fail-ings. Forms of devotion, forms of consolation.

I COULD REMEMBER when Yves first left the priesthood, and he brought Marguerite to our apartment to meet us. Sylvie had wondered whether it would be all right to curse in front of them or to mention smoking dope. "Absolutely," I said. In fact Yves came stiffly through the door in his tweed jacket, with his hands clasped behind him like a priest. Marguerite was so shy she would hardly take off her coat. They had, after all, just come out of years of lying about each other. Sylvie and I did our best to be irresistible and to draw them out—we told them our liveliest sto-ries, we fed them our most successful food, we had them tiptoe in to view the sleeping Marc. We were eager to pull them into the joys of coupledom. From our naturally elevated spot, we found the two of them quite charming, adorably embarking on an enterprise that was for us so familiar and durable.

I could not help feeling more advanced than Yves, who had taken so long to know that he needed what I already had. Sylvie was wearing a bright silk scarf around her hair and looked very pretty that night. How smug I was then. I watched her, as if I had invented her, out of my own cleverness; as if this were the only life I was going to have in this world, as if no others were waiting.

A NOTE ON SOURCES

In "The High Road" and "Gaspara Stampa," I have quoted directly from the poems of Gaspara Stampa, using the modern translations in Gaspara Stampa's *Selected Poems,* edited and translated by Laura Anna Stortoni and Mary Prentice Lillie (New York: Italica, 1994).

"Gaspara Stampa" also contains a passage from Petrarch's *Canzoniere,* translated into verse with notes and commentary by Mark Musa (Bloomington, IN: Indiana University, 1996).

For information on Gaspara Stampa, I have relied on Fiora A. Bassanese's *Gaspara Stampa* (Boston: Twayne, 1982). I was also helped by Patricia Fortini Brown's *Art and Life in Renaissance Venice* (New York: Harry N. Abrams, 1997).

"Ashes of Love" includes selected passages from *The Duino Elegies.* I have taken these from Rainer Maria Rilke's *The Selected Poetry,* edited and translated by Stephen Mitchell (New York: Vintage, 1989). The quote from Rilke's *Notebooks of Malte Laurids Brigge* is from the translation by Stephen Mitchell (New York: Vintage, 1985).

"Ideas of Heaven" is inspired by Eva Jane Price's *China Journal, 1889–1900: An American Missionary Family During the Boxer Rebellion* (New York: Scribner's, 1989). The character of Liz is my own invention but the details of her life in China owe much to these letters. I am also indebted to Nat Brandt's *Massacre in Shansi* (New York: toExcel, 1994, 1999). I owe special thanks as well to Li Xing Ye (Mark Lee) of Luoyang, Henan, People's Republic of China, for his conversation and letters about his experience with the Oberlin missionaries in Shanxi, and to his classmate, Raymond Chu, of Boulder, Colorado, for his translations and generous help.

"The Same Ground" is informed by the discussion of Marco Polo in Jonathan D. Spence's *The Chan's Great Continent: China in Western Minds* (New York: W. W. Norton, 1998), the book that also led me to Eva Price.